Finding Home

By Shelley Banks

Chapter One

Sophie yanked the driver's side visor down, but it didn't have the desired effect. The sun was blinding in its intensity, and the visor wasn't large enough to fully block the searing rays, a problem when she was trying to see the road in front of her. Although, not as much of a problem as the tears that refused to stop, no matter how many times she'd tried. It seemed that the waterworks were stronger than her resolve. She grabbed another tissue, dabbed her eyes, then threw it on the passenger seat, where it joined the other soggy, discarded reminders that she'd been crying since she'd left the chaos of the city. There had been so many tangled thoughts clogging her mind that it hadn't occurred to her to be better prepared for the long drive to her unknown destination. A water bottle would have been good, as would a rubbish bag, somewhere she could hide the sodden souvenirs of her state of mind.

With five hours still to go, she had to force herself to focus on the road ahead, not the one behind, and for a brief moment, she let herself feel the anger that had become part of her daily roster of emotions. Until, in a loud voice, she told herself to get a grip. This had been her decision, no one else had been involved, and she couldn't back out now. Even if she'd wanted to, there were no other options open to her that she wanted to consider; none that would give her what she needed. What she desired more than anything else was gone, and nothing could change that. The only choice she had was to continue down this road that was the first part of her new journey.

The physical road wasn't challenging—just one long, straight stretch of bitumen—it was the emotional road that was taxing. But even so, the vast emptiness on either side of the highway had the potential to lull her into a state of drowsiness. And she was already tired. So tired. Physically from packing. Mentally from the decisions that she'd been forced to make. Emotionally from the pain. She'd tried to keep the life she knew going, but eventually, she had to face reality.

The car was crammed with her possessions, things that were small enough to not require a place in the moving truck. Belongings that she didn't want to hand over to someone else to transport. Items of his she couldn't bear to part with, wasn't ready to not be surrounded by them.

The removalists had left the day before with the furniture and most of the boxes. She hadn't been able to watch as the two men went about their jobs, quickly and methodically, with no care as to what removing each piece from the house meant. Everything they picked up and carried outside were possessions that should have stayed exactly where they were. She kept wanting to yell out, to tell them to stop, but she stayed mute. They had no idea of the pain that pierced her heart every time another of the household items was moved from its rightful place and jammed into the truck, one on top of the other, taking up every tiny bit of space so everything would fit. So, she left them to continue, only speaking when one of them asked her a question. The only question she didn't answer was one about why she was moving. Instead, she'd pretended not to hear. That wasn't a topic she wanted to discuss with them, or anyone else. She'd told her family and friends that she was moving, using the minimal number of words to convey what was happening. And then she shut down any further conversation on the subject.

As she continued on, hands clenching the steering wheel to keep her on course, thoughts of last night floated into her mind. But instead of floating out again, the thoughts stayed, clinging like a barnacle and refusing to budge. It had been her last night in the house, and instead of sleeping, like she should have given the drive that would be in front of her the next day, she'd lain on a blow-up mattress and stared at the bare walls, the empty rooms reflective of her heart.

Sophie had loved the house from the minute they'd moved in. The light, airy rooms; the afternoon sea breezes that drifted in through the open windows; the enclosed verandah at the front where Tim had painted on weekends. The bookshelves in the lounge room, filled with the books she'd collected over the years, each one showing the signs it had been read more than once. The kitchen where they'd cooked together. The dining room where they'd hosted dinner parties. She wished she could keep it, but she could no longer afford it. She'd managed to last eight months on her own, but eventually the realisation that her funds didn't stretch far enough to continue to cover the mortgage could no longer be ignored. Those eight months had gone so quickly, she'd barely noticed that the days turned into weeks and then into months. She'd barely noticed anything at all.

As she'd locked the front door for the last time, she didn't cry, which surprised her. Nor did she cry when she dropped the keys off at the real estate office for the new owners to collect. She didn't cry in the car on the way out of the city either. The tears only started rolling down her cheeks when the distance between her old life and new one flipped the balance, with the old one now further away and the new one closer.

She was alone. As she would be from now on. She would never be able to replace Tim.

The further west she drove, the more desolate the landscape. Fitting really, she thought. Anything bursting with life would be to jarring; would not have matched how she felt. It was autumn, and the leaves on the few trees that she'd seen through the car window, all shades of orange, red, and brown, were trying to hang on to the branches for as long as they could before they would inevitably fall. It wasn't a stretch to compare herself to those trees. But even feeling the way she was, she did notice the colours. The leaves on the trees in the city didn't change like that. Here, to the north and west of her starting point, the climate was different. And it wasn't the only thing.

With another four hours in front of her, she didn't want to drive anymore. She wanted to turn around and go back. But there was nothing to go back to. No house. And no Tim. Her job in the local library would be there if she asked for it. As much as she loved being a librarian, a career she'd had for many years, she felt she needed to move to a different workplace. Not a big one; a similar job would be good. If she was going to move away, she'd have to find a new job as well. A lot of changes at once, but she felt she had no other option.

Which is how she'd found herself taking notice of the advertisement. Even though she knew she'd need a job to support herself, she'd found it hard to focus on the search for one. It had been hard to focus on much of anything. But one night, while aimlessly scrolling through job ads on the internet, one jumped out at her. It was at the bottom of the list, so far down it was likely to have been overlooked by others. She read it once and was about to close the browser when she decided to save the ad. Maybe she'd come back to it later. Maybe she wouldn't.

Three days later though, the ad was still floating around in the back of her mind, so she read it once more. She doubted the job would still be available, but she emailed her query anyway. And to her surprise, she got a response. From there, things had moved quickly, sometimes too quickly for Sophie. A job that led to a town; one she knew nothing about, but one that would suit what she was looking for at that moment in her life. A place where no one knew her, where no one would try to make things better when, no matter how hard they tried, they couldn't. A place where she could try to start again and hide from the world until she was ready to begin over. So, she found herself on a trajectory that pulled her along by its own will, which was good as she didn't have the energy to propel herself. A trajectory that led to her being in her car on this day, on this stretch of road, a long way from anything she was familiar with.

The road continued, long and straight. In the distance, she could see a service station, and when she reached the entrance, she turned in and parked in an empty spot. A coffee was what she needed, and a bottle of water, she reminded herself. As she hopped out of her car and glanced around, she noticed how tiny her vehicle was compared to the semi-trailers that lined the parking area to the side of the building. Insignificant and overshadowed, like her car could be swallowed up at any moment by large chunks of metal and rubber. She rushed inside to get away from that thought. The road was hard enough without thinking of the other vehicles that were traversing it, vehicles that knew the way, knew each kilometre of bitumen, almost as if they could find the way themselves without human intervention. This opposed to what she was doing—inching herself along at a snail's pace, unsure of the exact route of her journey and what she'd find when she finally reached her destination.

While she waited for her coffee, she looked at those around her. She was the only woman in the roadhouse and the only one not ordering food. Not that she was hungry, but even if she'd been, the deep-fried offerings in the hot box didn't appeal: chiko rolls, crumbed sausages, hot chips, potato gems, dim sims, battered fish, or something that looked like fish. Sophie didn't look close enough to see if it actually was, or if it was some unidentified, artificial substitute posing as fish, like the fish fingers she remembered eating as a child. The food on offer appealed to the truck drivers milling around, waiting for their orders. Although, out here, and if they'd been driving for hours and still had hours in front of them, they didn't have a lot of choice. Neither did Sophie, but the type of food in front of her would not sit well in her stomach, if she could get it down in the first place. She'd been spoilt for too long by Tim's cooking. Before meeting him, she'd never spent much time in the kitchen. But it hadn't taken long for his enthusiasm for creating dishes full of flavour to rub off on her.

She hadn't cooked anything since that fateful day, subsisting on sandwiches, cheese, and crackers and fruit. A diet, which, when combined with her grief, had caused her to lose weight, something she hadn't needed to do. Scrawny was probably the most appropriate description of how she looked. It wasn't the way she was used to her body looking, so to stop thinking about it, she avoided mirrors.

Beside her, one of the truck drivers tried to start up a conversation by asking her where she was heading. Out west was all she told him, before turning away. She wasn't in the mood for conversation, and besides, what else could they possibly talk about? She could ask where he was headed and what freight he had in his truck, but she wasn't interested in that. She wasn't interested in many things.

When her coffee was made, she headed back to the car, taking a few sips before she hopped in, enough to give her the boost she needed to continue. There was a long road ahead. And no one to go on the journey with her.

When it felt like she was close to her destination, Sophie glanced at the clock on the dashboard and was disheartened to see that only one hour had passed and she still had three hours to go. There was nothing appealing about the countryside she could see through the windscreen. Just more dry, brown land, dotted with infrequent, sparsely covered trees. She'd seen several kangaroos, and while usually, she would have been delighted by the sight of them, she was more concerned that one would make a sharp turn and jump onto the road and hit the front bumper of her car. She knew there were farms out here, but she hadn't seen them from the road, the houses to far back from the bitumen.

Inside the car, her possessions were squeezed into every available space, possessions that were well-suited to city life.

Like she was. What was she doing? Not for the first time, she thought that maybe she should turn the car around and head back, although to what, she didn't know.

That thought was still with her at two hours to go. At least in the last hour, she'd finally spotted a few farms. She hadn't spied any of the inhabitants, but the houses she'd noticed, standing at the ends of long driveways, almost as if they were standing guard to an entryway behind to another world, indicated there were people and not just more open lands for as far as she could see. And surrounding the dwellings, in fenced-off paddocks, she could see cattle, with the occasional dog or horse nearby. It turned her mind to wondering what sort of farms she would find dotted throughout her destination. Would they be cattle farms as she'd spied already? Or would they be something different? Having spent all her life in the city, she was aware of how important farms were and that without them, supermarket shelves would be empty. But she didn't have a great deal of knowledge about how farms operated. Maybe it was something she'd learn about. Considering her destination, it would be a good idea to find out. It was something that she hadn't thought to research while she was preparing for the change. A job and a house were all she'd looked into.

Not long after she passed the farms, she came to a small town and pulled over on the main street near a park to use the bathroom. There was a café across the road, and her stomach had decided now was the time to start growling. Her last meal had been breakfast, and while the food in the hot box hadn't appealed, maybe there were more options behind the café doors. She knew she had to eat something to keep her strength up, so she stepped inside.

'Afternoon', the male voice came from the back, behind the counter. 'We were just about to shut up shop.'

Sophie adjusted her eyes to the dimly lit café, the afternoon sun not strong enough to fully penetrate through the half-shuttered blinds. 'Oh, I can go.'

The man shook his head. 'We've still got plenty of food. What would you like?'

'A sandwich would be nice.'

'Ham and salad? Chicken and salad?'

Sophie thought for a moment. Which one did she feel like? She didn't really care which one, but her stomach was still rumbling, so she asked for the first option.

'One ham and salad sandwich coming right up.'

Sophie looked around her as he went into the kitchen. The tables and chairs were well worn, either because they hadn't been updated in a long time or because it was a very popular place.

'So, where are you off to at this time of the day?' he called out from the kitchen.

Sophie wondered for a moment how he knew she was off somewhere until she realised that he would know everyone in town.

'Heading further west,' she replied. As with the truck driver back at the service station, that was all she was prepared to say.

After she finished her sandwich, which was half the cost of the ones she was used to buying in the city but had double the filling, she walked through the park, noticing a family to her left. The two adults were holding hands, watching a child on the slippery slide. When the child reached the bottom, she giggled, then ran back to the stairs and climbed up again.

'Watch me again,' she called out as she sat at the top, ready to launch herself down the slide.

The couple looked so happy, their gazes turning from the child to each other and then back to the child. The man picked up the child when she reached the bottom, and the woman took a photo of them. She couldn't hear what they were saying, but they were all smiling.

Sophie kept her head down and strode by as fast as her feet would take her, tears threatening to spill down her cheeks. She didn't need to see the picture of what she thought her life was going to be. When she reached the toilet block, she hurried inside and shut the cubicle door behind her, staying there until she composed herself.

When she was done, she hurriedly washed her hands and walked swiftly back to her car, staring straight ahead, not making eye contact with the family nearby. She put them out of her mind as she pulled away from the kerb. Focusing on the road ahead, she resisted the urge to glance at the clock for as long as she could. When she finally gave in and glanced at the time, she felt the first stirrings of relief. Only an hour to go now. The thought of getting out of the car pleased her. Although the thought of arriving filled her with dread. This wasn't just a weekend visit. She was moving. It was a lot to take in.

She was so busy thinking about what this move really meant that it was the noise and not the visual that got her attention. A loud rumbling, almost like a growl. Startled, she looked in her rear-view mirror just in time to see a road train coming up behind her, so close now that she could only see the grill on the front. And then the indicator. It passed so quickly and so closely that her car shuddered, and it felt like she was being forced off the road. As the road train disappeared into the distance, she could still feel herself shaking so she pulled over, gripping the steering wheel tightly with both hands. The driver wouldn't have given her a second thought as he overtook. But in her small, appropriate for the city size car, she trembled. On the side of the road, hunched over the steering wheel, she finally let herself feel all the emotions that she'd been trying to keep shackled.

Sophie didn't know how long she stayed there, but when she felt like she'd gained control again, she pulled out onto the road and continued. She'd come this far. She couldn't turn back now. She just hoped that on the last part of her journey, there were no more road trains. Or happy families.

The final hour passed more quickly than the previous ones, and in the distance, she could see a sign. The words and numbers becoming clear as she got closer. Hillford 25 kilometres.

And another sign twenty-five kilometres later. Welcome to Hillford, Northwestern Queensland, Population 1563.

As she read the sign, Sophie wondered how often they changed the number on the sign. Would she be here long enough for the sign to reflect her presence?

Chapter Two

Sophie turned off the engine and rested her hands in her lap. After so many hours, she was pleased to let go of the steering wheel. Her shoulders ached from holding her arms in the same position. Staying in the driver's seat, she gazed at the house in front of her. The photos she'd seen didn't accurately show the scale, and the ivory timber dwelling was bigger than she'd thought. Far bigger than any other house she'd lived in; certainly bigger than the workers cottage near the beach she'd left behind only that morning. At least she wouldn't have to figure out how to make her furniture fit. Unless the rooms inside were many, and therefore poky, which she doubted, she'd have the opposite problem—empty spaces, much like her heart.

A wide verandah ran along the front, reached by four timber stairs rising from the earth, wrought iron railings encasing its length and sides. Behind the verandah stood three doors; a wooden, heritage red coloured front door in the middle, then at equal spans, on the left and right, two sets of French doors, with plain glass panels, giving access to whichever rooms were behind them. A crimson tin roof covered the structure, from the front to the back.

Structurally, it looked solid, but in Sophie's mind, her first impression was that the house had sense of tiredness about it. Much like her. Although in the case of the house, it just needed a few repairs and a general spruce up. Sophie would need much more than that. If only she knew where to start.

Sophie slid out of the car, placing her feet on the bitumen driveway. It took her a moment to stand and untangle her body from a posture caused by being confined to the driver's seat for so long. Once she had stretched and felt sturdy on her feet, she walked slowly down the left side of the house, around to the back, then up along the right-hand side.

The windows were casement, and a couple needed the hinges tightened. The ones in what she assumed were the bathroom and toilet from their size were frosted. Not that anyone would be able to see in anyway. There were no houses close enough where the neighbours would be able to peer in. The boards encasing the outside of the house could use a wash down, but apart from that, she couldn't see any sort of damage, just a few planks that needed extra nails. The space between the stumps the house was perched on and the dirt that ran underneath was bare.

Picking up the first of her belongings from the car, she hesitated before walking across the threshold, still not quite comprehending that this is where she would be living. Bags placed just inside the door, she began her inspection. Nothing a once over with a vacuum cleaner couldn't fix. Some repairs needed to be done inside too, but they looked minor. The vacuuming wouldn't be happening that day though. The drive had taken too much out of her, although the way she'd been feeling since Tim, she was surprised there'd been anything left to take.

As she came to the end of the tour, she decided that all she would do for the rest of that day was transfer her possessions from the car to the house, get something for dinner, and then have an early night. Thankfully, the removalists had put her furniture in the rooms they were intended for, and she had a bed to fall into.

On the kitchen bench, Sophie found a note welcoming her to the house, along with an apology from the owners about not getting the repairs done before she arrived. If she wanted to hire someone local to do the work, the owners would happily pay the bill. Under the note was a list which outlined everything Sophie had already noticed. As she read the note again, she thought about the Andersons, the owners of the house. She'd never met them as everything had been organised through email, including the location of the front door key which had been waiting for her, hidden under a rock in the garden. But she got the impression they were nice people and wanted her to be comfortable in their home. Some owners wouldn't have bothered and just expected her to live with things that needed fixing.

The car had finally been emptied of its contents, and, after unpacking the belongings she needed for that night, she reached for her phone to get dinner delivered, but her hand stopped mid-air. The places she and Tim had often ordered from on a Friday night when they were both tired after the working week were a long way away. No one was driving this far on their moped to drop off takeaway, no matter how many times they'd ordered from a particular restaurant before. One look through the kitchen window told her it was dark, and she doubted the only grocery store in town would still be open, so she couldn't even buy something easy to put in the oven.

With no other options available, she had no choice but to have a shower, put on some clean clothes, and head out to find somewhere to eat. Now that the stress of the drive was over, her hunger had returned, and the sandwich she'd consumed earlier no longer staved off the grumbling that was taking over her stomach.

Parking in town, she quickly discovered that her choices were the local pub or the RSL. The sounds coming from the pub were those of people who had been there for a while, so she opted for the RSL and its meal of the day—a $10 roast.

After ordering, she found a table in the corner, sat down, and looked around. Only a few tables were taken, but it was a Thursday night. She'd come to town a couple of days before she needed to start work to get acquainted with the place, although after arriving, she realised she needn't have bothered. The town was so small that she'd seen most of it already. She'd also seen the people at the other tables staring at her. They were trying to be subtle about it, but they weren't succeeding. She imagined they were all trying to figure out who she was.

The not-so-subtle looks while she waited for her dinner made her yearn for the local cafés she had frequented with Tim for breakfast on a weekend, with their crowds where she could blend in and eat without anyone looking at her. And where she could order something that wasn't just meat and three vegetables.

Sophie was examining the décor, which, by the look of it, hadn't been updated in twenty years, when a voice interrupted her thoughts.

'You must be the new bookstore manager.'

Sophie looked up and saw a man standing beside her table. She nodded. 'Yes, I am. How did you know?'

'Everyone knows everyone else around here, and you're the only new face we've had in town for a long time. Name's Jim.'

So, the looks she'd received hadn't been about wondering who she was. More likely, they were about checking her out.

Sophie looked up to see a man who she guessed was in his sixties, if the balding grey hair and wrinkles around his brown eyes were anything to go by. He still looked fit for his age, so Sophie assumed he was someone who'd worked on the land.

'Sophie,' she said.

'Welcome Sophie. It's a great town we've got here, and the people are friendly. All settled into the house?'

Sophie nodded again, reasoning that she shouldn't be surprised that he knew where she was living. 'Yes, I am. It's a nice house. I'll need to buy a couple of heaters though. I couldn't see any, and I imagine it gets cold here in winter.'

Jim concurred. 'Yes, it can get chilly. Head down to the Co-Op tomorrow morning and ask Len. He'll sort you out.'

'Thanks. I'll do that.'

As she watched Jim walk back to his own table, she noticed that he was eating alone too. Based on what he said about everyone knowing everyone else, he must have known the other diners. But for some reason, he'd chosen to eat by himself, and for a moment, Sophie wondered why.

Two other people stopped to introduce themselves. It was nice that they took the trouble to do that, but Sophie wasn't in the mood for company, or to provide any explanation of where she'd come from, why she was here, or how long she planned to stay. That last part she didn't even know the answer to. So as soon as she'd finished eating, she left before anyone else came over.

As she drove back to the house, she couldn't remember the last time she'd been surrounded by such darkness. Actual physical darkness. The emotional kind, she'd had plenty of experience with in recent times. It took her a moment to realise it was because there were no streetlights. Why she hadn't noticed that on the way to dinner she didn't know. But now it was all she could notice. At home, there were lights and noises everywhere. Not home, she reminded herself. That was gone.

When she pulled into the driveway, she was glad to see the lights she'd left on shining through the windows and on the verandah. A small beacon in the pitch black to help her navigate unfamiliar territory.

For the second time that day, she slowly climbed the stairs, but this time pausing on each tread to look up at the sky. Stars as far as she could see. The night sky was so clear, unencumbered by the glare rising from city lights or the smog coming from industrial estates. It was a mesmerising sight, and not one that she was used to. For a moment, a tranquil feeling washed over her, something that hadn't occurred since Tim. It didn't last long, but while it did, she hung on to it.

That night, it took Sophie a long time to drift off. As tired as she was after the drive, plus the past few days packing and sorting, it wasn't enough for slumber to come easily. The unfamiliar bed, the unfamiliar room. The silence was unsettling as well. Back home. No, she stopped herself for the second time that night. That would never be home again. Back in the city, she corrected herself, there was noise—cars driving by, trains in the distance, a dog barking in the street. Here, there was nothing. Not a sound. And the only thing she could see through the window was the moon, not full but not far off, its light adding a soft glow to the sky. She finally nodded off around 3 a.m. and woke at 9 a.m. She could have slept for longer, but the blanket she'd put on the bed to ward off the autumn chill last night was too hot now that the sun had been up for a few hours, and she woke with thin trickles of sweat on her body.

Even though she was awake, Sophie wasn't in a hurry to get out of bed. There was nothing to rush for. All that was in front of her that day was unpacking and stocking up on provisions. Neither of those things appealed to her as she lay there, staring at the walls and ceiling of the alien room, something she continued to do before her desire for caffeine outweighed her lethargy.

Rummaging through the box marked crockery, she found a mug. In the box marked pantry, she found the coffee and sugar. Thankfully she'd had the foresight to pick up a small milk when she'd stopped to get the sandwich the day before, along with a small bag of ice to keep it cold for the rest of the journey. All she had to do now was remember which box she put the kettle in. There were several boxes with kitchen appliances written across the top. As she stared at them, she'd wished she'd been more detailed in her descriptions. But packing had been hard enough without having to think of itemised explanations to scrawl in nikko pen above the strips of packing tape that held the lids of the boxes down.

As she rummaged through the boxes, images of where each appliance had been in the kitchen flashed through her mind. Memories of the last time she'd used them, mostly with Tim, who'd either been in the room with her or hovering somewhere nearby. He liked to be around her when they were both at home. We're both so busy, he'd say, it's nice to spend time together like this, even if we're doing something simple like making our lunches to take to work. With tears threatening to fall again, she shoved the boxes she'd already opened to the side, ripped the packing tape off the remaining one, and hunted through until she found the kettle, yanking it out and plugging it in. If only she'd chosen that box to open first.

Once the coffee was made, she took the cup outside onto the verandah and surveyed her surroundings, paying more attention than she had the afternoon before. To the right, she spied her nearest neighbour, but they weren't close enough that they'd be chatting over the fence. Or even calling out to each other from their yards. She was happy about that though, as she knew one of the first questions a neighbour would ask is how she'd come to move into the Anderson's place, and she didn't want to explain.

On the left-hand side of the house, she could see a large shed in the distance. Across the road, nothing but open paddock. The road she'd entered the property from the day before was bitumen, but only one lane with no kerb or channelling. The acre block that came with the house was bigger than anything she was used to, but it was small compared to those around her. She imagined that at one time, the house had been part of a farm, the land slowly being sold off piece by piece until only the house block remained.

The backyard was dotted with fruit trees, and there was a clothesline at the end of the concrete path that led from the backdoor. As she gazed around the yard, fully enclosed with wire fencing, she toyed with the idea of getting a dog. She'd wanted a dog for many years, but in the city, their block had been too small, and it wouldn't have been fair for the sort of dog Sophie would have bought if she'd had the possibility. Nothing too big, but she didn't want one of the small, fluffy, yappy kinds either. She wanted a breed that was medium size, one that she could easily manage but could still scare away unwanted visitors. And now, to also keep her company in this foreign place. The lack of space to keep a dog active was no longer a deterrent, so she kept the thought in the back of her mind.

Back inside, she did a more thorough inspection than she had the day before. Three large bedrooms and a sleepout in an enclosed section of the back verandah. Hardwood floors that once would have gleamed from the polish that had been applied many years ago but now faded because of the many pairs of feet that had trodden over it since it had been laid. The walls, painted eggshell, reached up to ceilings higher than those in a modern house. A large, spacious kitchen. Functional, not fussy. No gleaming benches or stainless-steel appliances. A kitchen that had seen meals cooked for families not dinner party guests.

As Sophie ran her hand across the laminate benchtops, she thought for a moment about pulling out one of the recipe books that were currently taped up in a box. Until she thought about the last time a meal had been prepared according to the instructions contained within the pages, Tim standing beside her. They'd mostly been his books. Once she started to cook more, always with Tim's encouragement because he'd loved it when they cooked together, she bought a couple of her own to add to their collection. They'd choose one of the new recipe books, try out the dishes they thought would be amazing, and the ones that were stayed on the rotating list they already had of meals they'd cook at night. The list grew longer each time they opened a new book. Sophie hadn't minded. It meant that there were months between repeating a dish, and she'd loved discovering new flavour combinations. Cooking since Tim's death consisted of preparing something easy to keep hunger at bay and nothing more.

To distract her from the memories swirling around in her head, she picked up her phone and read the advertisement again. 'Bookstore manager'. Those were the two words that got her attention. She'd never managed a store, but she knew a lot about books. For the past twenty years, she'd spent her days surrounded by them. Encircled by shelf after shelf. Row after row. Recommending books to her regulars. Waiting until they came back to return the book to ask if they'd enjoyed reading it. Happy when they did. Asking them questions when they didn't to help her pick another book they might like. But as much as she loved her job, she couldn't stay. Everyone knew what had happened, and she couldn't go in day after day and face their looks of care and concern, no matter how genuine. So, she began looking for another job.

In her search, she hadn't come across a job for a librarian advertised anywhere. And then she'd seen those two words—bookstore manager. She'd still be around books all day, so it wouldn't be too much of a change. And she'd still recommending books to read to those who came in. And the change of location might be good for her. Although as she looked around in that moment, maybe this new location was too much of a change.

Later that morning, Sophie hopped into her car and headed for the main street. She didn't take much notice of anything as she drove. She just wanted to get to the grocery store, buy some provisions, and head back to the house. She hoped she could duck in and out without any attention. Turned out, that was wishful thinking.

'Morning,' a cheerful voice called out as Sophie entered the store. 'You must be the new bookstore manager. I'm Maggie.'

She turned to the sound of the voice and saw a woman who looked to be in her early fifties, with auburn coloured hair and green eyes. She was about the same height as Sophie and looked like she kept herself fit.

Sophie nodded, wondering for a moment how Maggie knew who she was, before remembering Jim's words from the night before. 'Yes, I'm Sophie.'

'Can I help you find what you're looking for?' Maggie asked as she moved from behind the register, wiping her glasses with the front of her shirt as she did so.

Sophie nodded again. 'I don't have much in the way of food in the house, so I need to get some supplies, especially fresh food.'

Maggie smiled. 'Then you've come to the right place. I'll help you fill up the trolley. Have you got a list?'

Sophie handed over the grocery list she'd written, and Maggie proceeded to fill the trolley with fruit, vegetables, meat, a large bottle of milk, cheese, yoghurt, bread, and cereal. As Sophie watched her, she began to wonder if maybe it would be ok living here, if everyone was as friendly as Maggie.

'Did you just arrive in town?' Maggie asked, as she reached for a box of cereal from the top shelf.

'I got here yesterday afternoon, and from what I've seen so far, it seems like a picturesque place. I noticed a large hill as I drove in. There must be nice views from up there.'

Maggie smiled. 'There are. And that hill also gave us the town's name. Not very imaginative, but I guess the town's founders weren't big on creativity. Much more interested in running their farms.'

Sophie smiled too. 'At least they didn't have to look far for a name.'

Maggie laughed. 'And I assume they all agreed because I've never heard of any other suggestions that came up.'

As she continued to help Sophie with the groceries, Maggie pointed out where everything was so that next time, Sophie could easily find what she needed. As they walked up and down the aisles, Sophie wished she could find what she needed to mend her heart as easily as she could find the items on her list. She pushed those thoughts aside though. She wouldn't let Maggie see her tears. She didn't want anyone to see them.

Tim hadn't planned on going out that Saturday afternoon, but he'd been staring at the painting he was working on for what had seemed like an age without adding anything more to it. He'd told Sophie that he needed to go to the beach. He wanted to see the colours that would appear on the cliffs as the sun started its descent. Those were the colours he wanted to capture.

'I'll be an hour,' he'd said as he picked up the car keys.

When an hour turned to two, Sophie wasn't worried. She was used to Tim getting caught up when inspiration took over. Even at three hours, she continued with what she was doing. But at four hours, she tried ringing his number. Then again at five hours.

It was seven hours before the police knocked on her door. A drunk driver had swerved off the road and ploughed into Tim as he headed back to his car. Sophie had taken in all the policewoman said without responding. When the policewoman asked if she would be ok, Sophie nodded. And she was. Until the police car drove off. Then she slid to the floor and didn't move for the rest of the night.

Chapter Three

Sunday passed in a blur as Sophie unpacked one box after another. By the end of the day, she never wanted to see a cardboard carton again. Then Monday morning arrived far too swiftly for how she was feeling, and before she knew it, she was in the driver's seat, hands on the steering wheel. If only she could start the car. She already knew how far it was from the house to the bookstore thanks to her two previous trips into town. But she'd decided to leave a few minutes earlier to account for traffic. It was only once she was in the car that she remembered she wouldn't have to. She wasn't about to face the peak hour she was used to. That gave her a few more minutes to compose herself. Then she glanced in the mirror, applied some lipstick, took a deep breath, and pressed the ignition button.

Nine minutes later, Sophie parked on the main street in front of the bookstore. As she locked the car, she glanced around and was surprised at how many other cars were there. She'd thought the place would be quiet on a Monday morning, but it looked like she'd been wrong.

A few steps from the door, she stopped. Was she doing the right thing? Catherine had seemed lovely when Sophie had done the interview, but that had been online. Would Catherine be different face-to-face? It had been Catherine's calm and easy manner that had helped convince Sophie that maybe she'd be all right if she made the change from east to west. She was still going through the doubts in her mind when the door opened and Catherine beckoned her inside, a beaming smile spread across her face.

'I'm so glad you're here. I hope you got a park nearby. Monday is the day most of the farmers come into town for their weekly supplies.'

That explains the main street, Sophie thought to herself as she nodded in response to Catherine's question about a car park.

'I was just going to put the kettle on. Would you like a cuppa?'

Sophie nodded again, and a few minutes later, she was seated at one of the tables in the store with a cup of tea and a plate of biscuits in front of her. She was more of a coffee drinker, but tea sounded soothing.

'Did you have a good trip out?' Catherine asked as she sat down. 'It must have taken you a while to get here.'

'Yes, it was fine,' Sophie said, not wanting to go into details about the trip, nor how she'd been hoping that the further west she drove, the further away from everything that had happened she'd be, and the events of the past few months would be left behind. Turns out, it was a futile hope.

When Sophie had done the interview, she hadn't mentioned anything about Tim. All she'd said to Catherine was that she was looking for a change. A chance to try something different. She'd thought she'd sounded convincing, and Catherine hadn't asked anything else about her decision to move out west. But for a moment, as they spoke online, Sophie had thought she'd seen a look on Catherine's face. It had passed quickly though, so afterwards she decided she must have imagined it.

Catherine took a sip of her tea. 'Are you settling into the Anderson's place?'

'Yes, it's a lovely house,' Sophie replied, taking the easy answer for now. 'Much bigger than anything I've ever lived in before.'

'After the Andersons died, the parents that is, not any of the six children, I thought it would be sold. All the children moved into the city once they reached adulthood, like so many of the town's young people. But they decided to keep it.'

'It worked out well for me that they did,' Sophie said, although she wasn't sure if she'd ever feel at home there. Or even if she was going to stay. Something else she would keep to herself for now.

As soon as they'd finished their cup of tea, Catherine showed Sophie around the store. It was larger than she thought it would be, just like everything she'd come across so far.

'There aren't many entertainment options in town, so a lot of people read,' Catherine said, as if she knew what Sophie was thinking about the size of the store.

There were five tables including the one where they'd been sitting at the front of the store, to the left of the door. On the right, the bookshelves ran all the way down the side and around to the back wall. Behind the last of the tables stood a counter where people could pay for their books or order something from the food cabinet. The store didn't have an extensive menu—just sandwiches, wraps, and sweet treats—but all were homemade. Not by Catherine, she was quick to point out.

'Some of the other ladies in the CWA, mainly Bev and Jess, make them each day, and I give back some of the profits.'

Sophie nodded, hoping this arrangement would continue. Even though she could cook, she'd never been a baker.

The entire store was bathed in natural light thanks to the large, mahogany-coloured, timber framed windows that ran from either side of the door, which also featured glass panels, to the walls adjoining the stores on either side.

'Customers usually come in from opening time to around 10 am, mostly for coffee, because they're in a hurry in the morning,' Catherine said. 'Book sales are usually around the middle of the day when people come in for lunch and they've got a bit more time to browse. The people who work in town that is. If any of the farmers come in to buy a book, it's usually earlier in the day after they've finished all the business they need to do before heading back to their farms.'

Sophie looked around her at the books on the shelves. Books used to bring her comfort and joy. Overall, small and unassuming, but each book contained the keys to another world—people, places, and adventures. Every Monday morning, she used to get to work before the library opened and select the books she would read that week. This Monday morning, though, she didn't feel like picking up any of the books around her and reading the back covers.

Behind her, she heard the door open.

'Take a deep breath,' Catherine whispered to her, before turning around and facing the customer. 'Good morning, Harry.'

In response, Harry gave a slight nod of his head.

'The usual?' Catherine asked.

Again, Harry nodded. Sophie watched him while he waited for Catherine to make his coffee. He looked about Catherine's age, which Sophie knew was sixty-five. Like

Catherine, he had grey hair. His was cut short, what was left of it, while Catherine's was long and wavy and tucked behind her ears. He had brown eyes as opposed to Catherine's blue. Catherine was tall, and so was Harry. But while Catherine had a look of cheery disposition on her face, Harry just looked grumpy.

'Harry, this is Sophie,' Catherine indicated as she put the lid on his coffee cup. 'She's the new bookstore manager.'

'Don't see why you couldn't continue doing it,' Harry grumbled. 'You know I don't like change. Or new people in town.'

And with that, he picked up his coffee and walked out.

'Don't worry about him,' Catherine sighed, seeing the look on Sophie's face. 'He's like that with most people.'

'Why?' Sophie asked.

Catherine shrugged. 'I'm not one hundred percent sure, but I've got a theory. I'll share it with you someday. Right now, we need to get ready for the mid-morning rush.'

Sophie wondered what constituted a rush in a small town like this, and she was surprised when they sold sixteen coffees in twenty minutes. She expected only a couple of people to walk in. All sixteen introduced themselves, and all seemed nice. She didn't remember their names though. She'd been too busy learning how to work the coffee machine. She'd have to ask Catherine to give her a prompt when they came back in.

By the end of the first day, Sophie was exhausted. There had been so much to take in, and she was feeling overwhelmed. Not just with the store but with the move, the town, and the people. But at least she'd been busy, and that had dulled her emotions. Just a little.

And then there was Harry. He'd only been in the store for a few minutes, but it was enough for Sophie to know that he didn't want her there. In the store or in town. Would there be others like Harry? People who would be happy to see her go back in the direction she'd come from. The physical direction, that is.

And maybe she should. What was she doing here? Had her decision been too radical? If she'd waited a little bit longer, would she have found a new life in the city, one that she was happy with?

That night she went to bed early without cooking herself anything for dinner.

The following morning, Sophie arrived at the store earlier to help Catherine get things ready for the day. She'd been there about ten minutes when a woman walked in carrying a large, covered tray. She was tall and slim, with a build that indicated a life of physical work. Her grey hair was short, one of those cuts that required nothing more than a quick brush at the start of the day. Her skin was brown, but not the sort of colour that came from laying in the sun. Rather, it was the sort of that came from long days spent working on the land. She wore no make-up, and her blue eyes gave the impression that she'd seen a lot over the years. Her presence filled the room, and Sophie could tell straight away that she had a no-nonsense attitude and was someone who didn't tolerate fools.

'You must be Sophie,' she said, putting the tray on the counter. 'Catherine said you were starting this week. I'm Bev.'

'Nice to meet you, Bev,' Sophie said.

'Is Catherine here?'

Sophie nodded. 'She's out the back.'

'You can give me a hand with the sandwiches and slices then.'

Sophie pulled the cover off the tray and looked at the food. She could tell it had all been handmade in Bev's kitchen that morning.

'So, what brings you out here?' Bev asked. 'Catherine said you're a city girl.'

Sophie nodded again. 'Yes, I am.'

'This town will be different for you. Must have been a reason to leave the city behind and come here?'

'I got tired of the hustle and bustle,' Sophie said quickly. 'I wanted to try somewhere else. Somewhere quieter.'

Sophie hoped Bev wouldn't ask any more questions. It was too soon to mention Tim to anyone in town. If she ever did at all.

'You've picked the right place then,' Bev pronounced. 'No hustle and bustle here. And most people are friendly. There's one or two who are odd, but you get that anywhere. You'll know them when you meet them.'

'She's already met Harry,' Catherine said as she walked in from the office out the back.

'He's the oddest, so you can tick him off your list, Sophie.'

Catherine's eyes wandered from shelf to shelf in the cabinet. 'Everything looks delicious, Bev. What have you made today?'

'The wraps are chicken caesar, chicken and sweet chilli, and there's also plain salad. The sandwiches are roast beef, and ham and salad. Then there's passionfruit iced cupcakes, Mars bar slice, and carrot cake.'

Catherine looked at the food again. 'None of it will last long. I doubt there'll be anything left by the end of the day.'

'If there is, just put it to the side, and I'll give it to the farm hands. They don't mind if it's the day after.'

Then turning to Sophie, Bev told her she didn't like wasting food. And then she asked if Sophie was any good at baking.

'It's not something I've done a lot of. I more of a cook than a baker.'

As soon as she said it, she regretted it as those words triggered a memory of her and Tim in the kitchen, cooking the last meal they would ever prepare together. So, she was extremely grateful when Bev started talking again. This was not the time of place to let tears have free reign.

'Cooking is a handy skill to have. My mother taught me when I was a teenager.'

Catherine nodded. 'So did mine.'

'I know you grew up here, Catherine, but did you Bev?' Sophie said, wanting to steer the conversation on to a different topic.

Bev nodded. 'I've been here all my life. I've never had any desire to live elsewhere. I'm a farmer, my parents were farmers, so were my grandparents as well as my great-grandparents.'

Sophie was impressed. She'd never met anyone who continued in the family business for so long. 'Is it still the same farm?'

Bev nodded again. 'When my great grandparents arrived from Scotland, they didn't want to stay in Sydney, which is where the boat they came out on docked. They were from a small country town, and the city was too much for them. Although I don't know why they headed north to Queensland, towards the heat, rather than south towards the cold, given where they were from. Although, it does get cold here in winter.'

Catherne smiled. 'Probably not as cold as a Scottish winter.'

Bev laughed. 'No, not even close. But that's a good thing. The temperatures we get here are low enough for me. I wouldn't like anything colder.'

'Why did they leave and come to Australia?' Sophie asked.

'The usual story for the late 1800s—famine and poverty are why they left. They chose Australia because there was mass emigration from the United Kingdom at the time so, without knowing too much about the outside world, they followed everyone else.'

'Were they farmers in Scotland?'

Bev nodded. 'Sheep farmers, not cattle. But they learned the differences between the two quickly enough by all accounts.'

'And no one since then has thought about branching out to something else?'

Bev shook her head. 'We're a cattle farming area. That's what we know, so as far as I'm aware, no one ever thought of a different type of livestock, or even less likely, cultivating a crop. Some of my family didn't think the land was for them and they moved away. But at one time or another, they all came back. The land is in our blood.'

At the mention of the word blood, Sophie shivered. Controlled enough that Bev and Catherine didn't notice, although they were now in a conversation of their own. Blood made her think of Tim and how much there must have been when he was struck. She hadn't asked, and when the time came for her to make the identification, he looked like he was just sleeping. But she knew he wasn't. Instead of being in a bed, he was laying on a metal gurney, a sheet pulled up to his chin, hiding most of his body. There had been some minor bruising on his face, but the parts of his body that had taken the full impact, those were hidden from view. Not that she'd wanted to see. That would have added more horror to what she was already feeling. She'd just hoped it had been quick and he hadn't suffered.

Sophie glanced towards Bev and Catherine, and they were still in conversation. She used the moment to walk down one of the aisles to compose herself, pretending she was looking at the shelves. Tim was her story and not one she was willing to share.

'We'll have to get you involved in the CWA after you've settled in,' Bev called out, bringing Sophie back to present. 'We have a cooking committee that puts meals together for when people are going through a rough patch.'

As Sophie exited from the bookshelves and made her way back to the counter, she wasn't sure what Bev meant by a rough patch, and she wasn't sure she should ask. She must have had a puzzled look on her face because Catherine told her a lot of people were enduring hardship because of the drought.

Coming from the city, Sophie didn't know much about the drought. Only what she saw on television. But she felt she should. So, she listened to Catherine and Bev as they talked about the farmers in the area. Their friends. Listened as they talked about there not being enough food for the animals. About the cost of trucking in water, which many struggled to pay. About houses being re-mortgaged to get extra money. And how sometimes that couldn't be paid back.

'We support everyone as much as we can,' Catherine stated. 'Everyone in town does. But it's often not enough.'

Bev nodded. 'Let's hope we get rain this year.'

As she headed towards the door, Bev turned to look at Sophie. 'Why don't you try a few of the things I've brought in today? You look like you could use some good nourishment.'

Sophie tried to stop the look that was spreading across her face, but she was unsuccessful.

Catherine smiled. 'Don't mind Bev. She's like a mother hen. Always wanting to make sure everyone is all right. She doesn't mean anything by it.'

Sophie nodded.

'And I must say, I agree with her. A little more meat on your bones would do you good.'

Sophie couldn't deny that. Nourishment was something that had been lacking lately. Physically and emotionally.

For the rest of the day, the drought was in the back of Sophie's mind. Maybe she could do something to help. It would be nice to do something for others. And to think of others rather than her own grief.

That night though, she didn't think about the drought. Or the town. She was unpacking the last of the boxes, and she came across the one she'd been putting off. The one that contained tangible memories of Tim. Sophie stared at the box for a moment before slowly peeling back the tape on the lid. On top, tied in a bundle by a ribbon, were all the cards Tim had given her. He'd always put a lot of thought into which card to get and the words he filled them with.

Underneath the cards were a series of framed photos. Photos of the two of them on holidays, dressed up to go out, one taken in front of the house they'd shared.

Under the photos was a painting. Of her. Tim had painted it not long after they'd started going out. It perfectly captured the hazel flecks in her eyes and the soft waves in her light brown hair. When they'd moved in together, he'd hung it up in the dining room. She'd felt uncomfortable at first when people came over. But he'd said he wanted everyone to see how important she was to him. Here, in this house, she put the painting back in the box along with the other items and closed the lid.

What she needed was some company, just not the humankind.

Chapter Four

As she drove, further out of town than she'd ventured so far, the quiet roads were something she wasn't used to yet. She'd only seen three other cars in the fifteen minutes she'd been driving. Apart from those, her company was kilometre after kilometre of grassy paddocks and grazing cows. It was peaceful, she had to admit, but she would have preferred something to distract her from her thoughts—more cars, people, noise—anything but the silence.

The closer she got to the address she'd been given, the more she began to wonder if it was the right time to take on such a big commitment. If she was going to change her mind, she needed to do it now. But somewhere in her mind, a thought lodged itself. This would be good for her. So, she didn't turn around and kept driving towards her destination.

As she turned into the property and headed down the long gravel driveway towards the house, she couldn't see anyone around. So, she parked and headed for the front door. And then behind her, she heard a noise and turned to see a puppy bounding across the grass. The roly poly bundle screeched to a halt at her feet and then tried to clamber up her legs, its tail wagging furiously.

'I think she likes you,' a voice called out.

Sophie turned in the direction it was coming from and saw a man about her age walking towards her.

'I'm Ryan,' he said, extending his hand.

'Sophie,' she replied.

The man in front of her was taller than she was, which wasn't hard as Sophie stood at only 160 centimetres. He had brown hair, brown eyes, and was in very good shape, either from a physical job or spending time in the gym.

Sophie shook his hand and introduced herself before turning her attention back to the puppy. She didn't know a lot about Border Collies, but she knew this one was adorable. With a black and white coat, floppy ears, and a tiny pink tongue, the tip of which was showing, Sophie was captivated. It only took one look into the puppy's eyes to realise the feeling was mutual.

'She's quite taken with you,' Ryan said. 'I think you might have got yourself a dog.'

Sophie picked up the wriggling puppy and almost immediately, it started snuggling into her. Whatever earlier hesitation she'd had was completely gone. 'I think I might.'

'She'll need plenty of exercise,' Ryan said, giving the puppy a pat on the head. 'She's a working dog.'

Sophie paused for a moment. She hadn't thought about that. A working dog might be too much for her. But as she looked at the puppy, her heart continued to melt. For the first time since Tim had passed away, she started to feel love trickling into her heart. Not the sort of love she would have felt for a person. But enough that she knew that no matter how much work the puppy would be, the adorable, wriggling bundle in her arms was exactly what she needed.

'I'll have to check the fence when I get back, just to make sure she can't get out,' Sophie said as she placed the puppy back on the ground.

She tried to do it gently, but the puppy launched herself out of Sophie's arms about thirty centimetres above the grass. She was so excitable that she tumbled and rolled and then ran around in circles in front of Sophie.

'If anything needs fixing, I can do that for you. As well as being the local mechanic, I'm also the local handyman.'

'That's good to know,' Sophie said, remembering the note that one of the six remaining Andersons had left her. 'There are a few things at the house that need fixing. Would you be able to come and have a look?'

'I can come over tomorrow after work if that suits you.'

Sophie nodded. 'That would be great. Thank you.'

'Take some more time and play with the puppy, just to make sure you're happy to take her. I'll be in the shed. Just yell out when you're ready.'

As Sophie watched Ryan walk away in the direction of the very large tin structure, she felt something on her leg. Looking down, she saw the puppy, jumping up and down, trying to crawl up her leg again. She reached down and picked up the puppy for the second time. The look of unconditional love as she gazed up at Sophie made her heart melt. This was just what Sophie needed. And a dog that needed plenty of exercise would be good too. It had been a while since Sophie had done any form of exercise, unless packing and unpacking counted. With the puppy, she could get into the habit of daily walks, something that would be good for both of them.

On the way home, Sophie stopped and bought supplies. A bed, food, water bowl, and several toys for the puppy to play with, along with the flea and heartworm tablets Ryan said she'd need. As she looked down at the toys, she hoped they'd be enough to distract the puppy from chewing anything else. She'd done some research online about training puppies before she'd headed out this morning so she wouldn't be completely clueless if she decided the puppy was for her. And Ryan said he'd be happy to answer any questions she had or offer advice. He seemed genuine about helping, which was nice. Although everyone she'd met so far had been like that. Except Harry of course, but she'd already decided to avoid him as much as possible. There was something about Ryan that she couldn't put her finger on though, almost like underneath his friendliness, there was a barrier that he put up between himself and others. Or maybe that was just with her, seeing as she was new and he didn't know her.

As soon as she got back to the house, she planted herself on the front stairs and watched the puppy as it gambolled across the yard, stopping to sniff everything she came across. The pure joy she was witnessing made Sophie smile. She still hadn't come up with a name though. None of the ones she'd thought of during the drive back seemed to suit the adorable creature. She needed to come up with one quickly though. She couldn't just keep calling her 'puppy'.

The following afternoon, after being on her feet all day at the bookstore, Sophie felt weary as she pulled up at the gate. But there, on the other side, was a very small border collie, a look of joy plastered all over her face. It was as if seeing Sophie come home was the best thing that had ever happened. And instantly, Sophie felt the weariness disappear.

She picked up the beautiful pooch, popped her on the front seat, and drove through the gate. She was glad she wasn't driving fast or had too far to go as the puppy didn't stay on the passenger seat, instead crawling over onto Sophie's lap and licking her face.

As soon as she parked the car and opened the door, the puppy jumped out, then turned around to make sure Sophie was following, her tail wagging the whole time. A smile spread across Sophie's face, and against her better judgement, she sat down on the ground and let the new addition to her life crawl all over her. The puppy was warm and soft, and also, very wriggly. But Sophie stayed where she was until a cramp began to spread across her right foot, and she got up before it got any worse.

Once inside, Sophie looked at her watch. Ryan would be arriving soon. She made herself a coffee, which she sipped while going over the list. If Ryan was kind enough to come over and do the repairs, the least she could do was be prepared for his arrival.

'Does she have a name yet?' Ryan asked, picking up the puppy as he hopped out of his ute.

Sophie shook her head. 'I've thought of a few, but I'm not happy with any of them. I need to come up with something that suits her.'

'She's a beautiful dog,' Ryan said. 'She needs a beautiful name.'

Sophie nodded. 'Yes, she is beautiful. And so full of love.'

'It's a shame people aren't always like that.'

The look on Ryan's face let her know that he'd said something he hadn't intended to. He turned to stare at the yard for a few moments and then asked Sophie to show him what needed to be repaired. Then, before she had the chance to answer, he walked inside. Sophie watched him go, assuming she was supposed to follow. Why had Ryan said what he had? And what else would he have said if he hadn't stopped speaking so abruptly?

As they walked through the house, Sophie pointing out the things on the list that needed to be fixed, she wondered why she was interested in knowing what else he might have said. She couldn't pinpoint the reason, but nevertheless, she wanted to know.

After they'd covered everything and decided on days and times for Ryan to come and do the work, he departed. As Sophie watched him leave, there was something else she was now thinking about. There was something under that exterior, something she couldn't put her finger on. And for the second time in a short period, she pondered over why she was curious.

The next morning, as she watched the puppy through the window while she waited for the jug to boil, it came to her. Molly. She didn't know what made that particular name pop into her head, but the moment it did, she knew it was perfect. When she'd made her coffee, she took it outside and sat on the verandah.

'Molly,' she called.

The puppy, who was keeping herself entertained by rolling around in the front yard, stopped at the sound of Sophie's voice and stared, her head titled on a slight angle, as if she was puzzled.

'Molly,' she called again.

The puppy hesitated, not familiar with the name.

But the third time Sophie called out, Molly bounded over in her usual rambunctious way. Her puppy now had a name. It gave her something to smile about as she drove to the bookstore. Unfortunately, the smile didn't last very long after she arrived.

'It's you,' a voice said as the door to the bookstore opened. 'Where's Catherine?'

When she turned around, she could see Harry heading towards the counter.

'She's gone to the post office,' Sophie said. 'She'll be back soon.'

Harry sat down at one of the tables. 'I'll wait.'

'Can I get you anything?'

Harry shook his head. 'I want a coffee, but I'll wait until Catherine gets back.'

'I can make you one.'

Harry shook his head again. 'I only like the ones Catherine makes. You'll do it wrong.'

Sophie was going to say she was perfectly capable of making a coffee but thought the better of it.

'Why are you here anyway?' Harry asked.

From the tone of his voice, Sophie could tell he wasn't asking out of curiosity. He didn't seem pleased she was there. She decided to ignore his question.

Ten minutes later, Catherine still wasn't back.

'I can't wait around all day,' Harry said. 'You'll have to make my coffee. Try to do it right.'

Sophie focused her attention on the coffee machine so she wouldn't say something she might regret. Why was he so rude?'

'Here you go,' Sophie said in a cheery voice that she had to fake.

Harry took one sip and then put the cup back on the counter.

'I knew you'd do it wrong.'

'What's wrong with it.'

'It doesn't taste like the ones Catherine makes.'

'It's the same coffee, same milk, and the same coffee machine.'

'Well, I don't know what you've done then. It's terrible. You city people don't know how things are done in a town like ours.'

'I'm pretty sure we make coffee the same way. I'm not from a different country. Not even a different state.'

'You should have stayed where you were. We don't need strangers in town.'

Sophie watched as he walked out the door after saying that. She couldn't believe how awful he'd been. And how much it wounded her.

She was still feeling dismayed when Catherine came back. Harry's words had been unkind, but it was more than that. Ever since she'd awoken that morning, her thoughts had been filled with Tim and the life they had together. Images of places they'd been and things they'd done together drifted through her mind. She wanted that life back. All of it. She didn't want to be in this town. Didn't want any of this to be happening. And the things Harry had said only reinforced those thoughts. But she didn't tell Catherine any of that, only about her interaction with Harry.

'He's such a grumpy old man. I'm going to say something next time I see him.'

Sophie shook her head. 'You don't have to do that.'

'Yes, I do. I'm not letting him get away with talking to you like that. You are most certainly welcome in this town, and we're better for your presence. Now, forget what he said, and I'll make us a cup of tea.'

Sophie tried to do what Catherine said, but Harry's words stuck with her for the rest of the day. As did the thoughts of the life she used to have.

That afternoon, as Sophie got out of her car, she noticed something laying in the yard. It wasn't until she got closer that she saw it was one of her towels. One that she'd put on the clothesline that morning. One that had obviously been too much of a temptation for Molly.

As soon as Sophie eyeballed her, Molly knew she'd done the wrong thing, crouching low to the ground, as if she was trying to make herself disappear. But the look on Molly's face meant that Sophie couldn't stay mad, instead picking her up and letting her snuggle into her arms. She knew it was the wrong thing to do. She should be disciplining Molly instead. But after her run-in with Harry, a puppy cuddle was exactly what she needed. Animals were so much simpler than people. The only thing Molly gave her, apart from ripped towels, was unconditional love. Something she once had but was now gone forever.

Later that night, with nothing on TV to distract her, she opened one of the boxes that contained her books. There were still several boxes that remained taped up. Ones she hadn't been in the right frame of mind to open.

She and Tim would regularly spend hours at night, sitting on their verandah, rugged up in winter, a fan blowing in summer, reading beside each other. Often, they wouldn't notice how much time had passed, both engrossed in what they were reading. She'd enjoyed those nights. Something so simple, and yet, so special.

Sophie hadn't read anything since he'd gone. And looking down into the box, she knew she wasn't ready to start again. Instead, she went to bed, not tired yet but not wanting to rattle around the house by herself. And she put Molly on the bed beside her.

It wasn't something she'd planned on doing when she'd first bought Molly home. But that night, in the darkness and stillness, the sound of the puppy breathing and occasionally, the little snore that escaped from her mouth, made Sophie feel less alone.

When she woke the following morning, Molly was still in the same spot she'd been when Sophie had finally fallen asleep. She looked so adorable that Sophie didn't want to wake her. But as soon as Sophie tried to move, Molly woke up and immediately crawled on top of her body and started licking her face. Sophie lifted her up and gazed at her puppy. From the look on Molly's face, she realised she'd started something she shouldn't have, but it didn't bother her as much as she thought it would. Anything that made her smile right now, she was happy to go along with. Even if it didn't last very long.

As much as she would have liked to stay tucked under the covers all day, that wasn't a realistic option. She stretched her arms above her head, yawned once, then climbed out of bed, shivering unexpectedly as she threw the blankets off. Overnight, it felt like it had changed from autumn to winter, even though that season didn't officially start for another couple of weeks. Winter wasn't Sophie's favourite; she was much more of a summer person, so she wasn't looking forward to the next few months.

Before venturing to the front door so she could let Molly out, Sophie reached for a jacket, wondering as she did if she had enough clothes appropriate for the country winter chill. Catherine had already told her it was colder out west than it was near the coast. As she walked outside, Molly bounding behind her, she pulled the jacket tighter, the chill going right through her. Catherine had been right, although as Sophie was beginning to realise, she always was. The temperature didn't seem to be bothering Molly though as she wandered through the front garden, squatting occasionally to mark her territory, then, as she continued on, sniffing everything she came across as her tiny paws trotted across the frost-covered ground. Sophie watched her, and the simple pleasure Molly was getting from exploring the garden helped settle her mind.

But after a while, the bracing air became too much, and she called Molly and went back inside. She still had an hour before she had to leave for the bookstore, time she could have used for something productive, but she just couldn't find the energy. Everything was still too strange, unfamiliar. There was nothing yet that made her feel like she belonged where she was. Had she made the right decision?

She was still pondering that question as she parked her car outside the bookstore later that morning.

The first thing she needed to do, before she forgot, was unwrap the book that had been delivered for one of their regular customers. It hadn't been in stock, so Catherine had ordered it. The purchaser was coming in that morning to pick it up, and Catherine had ducked out, so Sophie was the one getting it ready for sale. As the last of the wrapping came off, she froze. It was one of Tim's favourite books. Before she could stop herself, tears began streaming down her cheeks. And then the door opened, and Sophie didn't have time to hide before Bev was standing right in front of her.

'What's wrong?' Bev asked, putting down the tray she was carrying and pulling Sophie into a hug.

And so, once she had the tears under control, Sophie told someone in town about Tim.

'You poor thing,' Bev declared, hugging her more tightly. 'What a terrible thing to go through, especially on your own.'

The door opened again, and this time, Catherine walked in. 'Is everything all right?'

Sophie shook her head before extracting herself from Bev's arms and repeating what she'd just shared.

Catherine then inserted herself in the spot Bev had only just relinquished and put her arms around Sophie. 'I knew there was something. I can't imagine going through something like that.'

Sophie dried her tears and turned to look at Catherine. 'But your husband passed away.'

Catherine nodded. 'Yes, but he was ten years older than me, so he when he died last year, he was seventy-five. And his health had declined in recent years, so it wasn't unexpected. Not like what happened to you.'

Sophie thought about what Catherine said. The unexpectedness of Tim's passing was one of the hardest things to get her mind around. She'd thought they had many years ahead of them. But it turned out she'd been wrong.

As the day progressed, Sophie was grateful that it was busier than she'd experienced so far. It kept her busy, and it stopped her from thinking about her revelation to Bev and Catherine. She hadn't planned on telling anyone about Tim. Now that others knew, she felt vulnerable, an emotion she didn't want to add to all the others that had taken hold at various times since the day she wished had never happened.

As one person after another came in, chatting as they made their purchases, Sophie's mood started to lift. Every person she talked to was friendly, and for those she hadn't met before, they were also welcoming, something Sophie appreciated. In the back of her mind, a thought started to form, one that concerned her decision to come to Hillford. Yes, Harry had been awful, but he was the only one who had been. She wasn't a particularly spiritual person, but that day, she felt like someone was watching out for her, providing her with exactly what she needed.

But by mid-afternoon, she was weary, the weight of sharing what happened to Tim settling over her. Catherine must have realised as she kindly offered to lock up so Sophie could leave earlier than she was supposed to.

As she drove back to the house, for some reason, she thought about her first serious boyfriend, someone she hadn't thought of in years. They'd met at a mutual friend's birthday celebration. Matt had been the life of the party, keeping everyone entertained and laughing. Sophie had been quieter back then, shy. It had taken her another couple of years to fully come out of her shell.

She'd been so young when she and Matt first got together, only nineteen, and she didn't really know what to expect from a relationship. But they'd been together for seven years, and she'd thought that they would continue as they were and that this would be her life from now on. When things ended, she hadn't known what to do or how to deal with her first broken heart. Then she'd met Tim, and it didn't take her long to realise he was the one. And now her heart was broken for a second time. This time though, it wasn't just broken. It was shattered into a thousand pieces. She couldn't imagine there would ever be another person, as there had been after Matt. No one could ever take Tim's place.

As she pulled into the driveway, she spotted Ryan's car, remembering only then that he'd said he'd be arriving around 2.30pm. After the events of the day, she was in no mood for company and wished she'd thought about it earlier and cancelled. Instead, she hopped out of her car and greeted him.

'Hello to you too,' Ryan said. 'I started some of the outside work while I was waiting for you to arrive.'

Sophie nodded in acknowledgement.

'The door was locked so I couldn't start anything inside,' he said, following her up the front stairs.

'Was I meant to leave it unlocked for you?'

Ryan shook his head. 'No one locks their doors around here, so I didn't think to mention it.'

For someone who'd always lived in the city, leaving doors unlocked was something she'd never done, much less thought of.

Ryan could see the puzzled look on her face. 'I guess you're not used to that. You don't have to leave the door unlocked if it makes you uncomfortable.'

Sophie shook her head. She had to start coming to terms with the different way things were done here, and once she'd successfully done that, she needed to replicate that in her behaviour without being prompted.

'I'll leave the door unlocked next time.'

Sophie opened the door and headed inside, thinking the best thing she could do was stay out of his way. But he followed her, toolbox in hand, and began work on the inside of a window frame, the same one that he'd just finished fixing on the outside.

'How was your day at the bookstore?' he called out, seemingly happy to talk while he worked.

'It was fine. Nothing out of the ordinary.'

It was lie, but he wouldn't know that. She had no intention of discussing what she'd shared with Bev and Catherine. Two people knowing was enough for one day, enough for the foreseeable future as far as she was concerned.

'How are you settling in?'

'So far so good. This is a lovely house, the bookstore is great, and I've met some very nice people since I've arrived.'

That wasn't the whole truth, but the whole truth was too complicated, and it wasn't something she wanted to go into anyway. How could she explain her uncertainty about being here in the first place without going into the reason why she was here? After the events of the day, all she wanted to do was be alone. Even Molly bouncing around all over the place felt like too much.

Although she felt like she was being rude, she excused herself and told him she was taking Molly for a walk. She'd tried putting the lead on a couple of times without much success, but she needed to persevere. While there was plenty of room for the puppy to run around the yard, if Sophie wanted to take Molly somewhere, she would need to go on a lead.

As they set off down the driveway, Molly was all over the place, pulling left then right, then running around in circles, not listening to anything Sophie was saying. She deliberately didn't turn around and look back at the house because if Ryan was watching, she didn't want to know. If he was looking at her, he'd probably be thinking that city people didn't know how to handle dogs. She decided when they got back, she'd do more research online about how to train a puppy.

Sophie didn't have a destination in mind. She just wanted to walk, to clear her head as well as get some exercise for herself and the energetic bundle in front of her. She wasn't sure how long she walked for, not wearing a watch nor bringing her phone, but when the sky turned from day to night, she turned around and headed back. Even Molly was a little tired by now. It probably wouldn't last though, and she'd be running around again after a brief rest.

As she walked up the driveway, she could see that Ryan's car was gone.

Chapter Five

'Morning,' Jess called out as she walked through the door. 'Here's the food for today.'

Sophie looked down at the tray Jess had placed on the counter. 'It all looks delicious.'

'Thanks. Hopefully, it tastes delicious as well.'

Having already enjoyed the food Jess had brought in so far, Sophie knew it would.

'There'll be nothing left by the end of the day, and on the off chance there is, it won't go to waste,' Sophie said with a grin while patting her stomach.

Jess laughed. 'Next time I'm on the baking roster, I'll bring in extra, just for you.'

When all the offerings were in the cabinet, Sophie handed the empty tray back to Jess.

'Have you got any plans tonight?' Jess asked.

Sophie shook her head.

'Why don't you come over for dinner?'

'I'd like that.'

'Great. Come over around 6.30 pm.'

'What would you like me to bring?'

'Just yourself. See you then.'

Sophie watched as Jessica headed out of the shop. It would be nice to have dinner with someone instead of eating by herself, with only the TV on in the background so she didn't feel completely alone. At least over the past couple of weeks, she'd began making more of an effort with the food she prepared for her meals, and it was showing. She looked healthier than she had when she first arrived in town, and she had more energy too. It was a nice change and helped balance out the ever-present pain.

She'd first met Jess, one of the local schoolteachers, not long after arriving in town, and had slowly gotten to know her. Every time she dropped food into the store, Jess stayed and chatted for a while before heading on her way. She was closer in age to anyone else Sophie had met so far, except Ryan, and Sophie relished their conversations. As much as she enjoyed spending time with Catherine, and with Bev when she came in, she felt like she had things in common with Jess. Expect the obvious. Jess was married, with a lovely husband and a beautiful son. Sophie had no one.

After Jess left the store, a flurry of customers came in and out, taking their coffees, treats, and occasionally, a book with them. The pace continued to be steady all morning, so it was lunchtime before Sophie opened the box containing that day's delivery.

One of their customers had ordered a copy of *The Jane Austen Book Club* by Karen Joy Fowler, and as she stared down at the book, an idea popped into her mind.

'Has there ever been a book club in town?' Sophie asked as she contemplated the cover.

Catherine looked up from what she was doing and shook her head. 'I've thought about starting one a few times, but I never got around to organising anything.'

'Do you think there would be any interest if I asked around?'

Catherine nodded. 'I think you'd get a few takers. Lots of avid readers in the area. As you're starting to become aware of thanks to our regular customers.'

Sophie continued to think about it as she unwrapped the other orders and either put them on the shelves if it was a book she or Catherine had ordered for the store, or in the pile to be picked up if it had been ordered on behalf of a customer. Ordering books online and having them delivered to their homes was not something the townspeople had taken too. They preferred to buy their books the way they always had, the way that supported Catherine and her small, local business.

A book club. It would be a good way to do something social without the pressure of having to talk about herself. The time would be taken up chatting about whichever book was up for discussion. And it could be held in the bookstore, meaning no one would have to come to the house she was living in. Holding it at the house would only provide another opportunity for questions about her life and how she came to be in Hillford.

She'd called it her house a couple of times since she'd moved in, but that was more out of habit than anything else. It certainly didn't feel like her house, even though her possessions were in every room. But her belongings had just been plonked down in any space they fit. There was nothing thoughtful about where things had been placed.

The more she contemplated the idea of a book club, the more convinced she became that it was something she should pursue. It would keep her occupied while she was here, however long that would be. And it would get her reading again, something she missed dearly. She found herself smiling, something else she hadn't done for a long time. Unfortunately, the smile didn't last. But not of her own choosing.

'I haven't seen you for a while,' Catherine said as the door to the store opened, the tone in her voice so clear that anyone would be able to pick up on it.

'I've been busy,' Harry said.

'Busy? More likely you've been staying away because you knew I'd be cranky with you.'

'What for?'

'For what you said to Sophie.'

'I didn't say anything.'

'Yes, you did. I heard all about it.'

'It was nothing.'

'You left her in tears.'

Harry was about to say something, but the look on Catherine's face stopped him.

'You need to apologise.'

The look on Catherine's face was still there, and Harry knew that if he wanted to keep coming into the store, he didn't have a choice but to do what was asked of him.

Harry sat down. 'You could at least make me a coffee.'

'I'll make one, but in the meantime, don't you have something to say to Sophie?'

He didn't change his position, nor did he change his focus from Catherine to Sophie.

'Harry?' Catherine prompted after a few moments when he hadn't said anything.

Harry turned his eyes away from Catherine and looked towards Sophie. 'Catherine said I upset you.'

Sophie nodded.

'I didn't mean too. Sorry.'

Sophie watched him as he said it. She could tell he wasn't going to say anything else, but the expression on his face was genuine, as was the tone he used, and together those two things convinced her that he'd meant what he said, even though he'd been coerced into saying it.

'Thank you.'

Then Harry looked away and kept quiet until his coffee was ready.

'I've got places to be, so I'll see you both next time,' Harry said as he headed towards the exit, beverage in hand.

As the door closed behind him, Sophie turned to Catherine. 'Do you think he really has places to be?'

Catherine shook her head then smiled. 'I think he just wanted to leave as quickly as he could.'

Sophie smiled as well. 'That's what I thought too.'

And with that, Sophie put Harry out of her mind.

But as soon as she left the store that afternoon, the words he'd apologised for came back to her. She was a stranger, and even though she'd received a warm welcome from others she'd met, maybe she always would be. She wasn't from this town, didn't grow up here, didn't have several generations of farmers in her family history. She was different.

Given everything that had happened, she wanted to belong, wanted to be part of something. That was one of the reasons she'd settled on Hillford in the first place. In her internet research, she'd come across an article saying it had received the friendliest town award the year before, and that appealed to her. She told herself that it was only Harry so far who hadn't been friendly. But what if there were more like him?

What she needed was something to replace Harry's words in her mind. Something she found as she pulled into the driveway and hopped out of the car. Molly came bounding towards her, the look of joy on her face was enough to push all other thoughts away. Sophie picked up the squirming bundle and cuddled her for a long time, wanting to keep hold of the affection her puppy was providing.

An hour later, Sophie found herself staring at the contents of her wardrobe, trying to decide what to wear to Jess' house. She vetoed several outfits because they were either too dressy or too casual, before deciding to go with one of her dresses. She hadn't worn a dress since she'd arrived, and it would be nice to put one on again. Just not one she used to wear when she went out with Tim on their date nights.

Even though they'd been together for several years and had lived together for most of them, Tim still made a point of having regular date nights. He picked places they hadn't been before, so they always got to try something new.

Sophie loved their date nights. Sometimes they'd get dressed up and go somewhere fancy, with candlelight and waiters who scrapped the crumbs off the table. Other times, they'd get takeaway and sit in a park or at the beach, and on those nights, Tim always made an extra effort, bringing their folding table and chairs, a tablecloth, and plates and cutlery so they didn't eat out of takeaway containers. The last date night they'd had together was a night like that. Tim had heard about a new Vietnamese restaurant which had been getting great reviews. Instead of sitting inside, which had been decorated with all the stereotypes you'd expect to find including a wall completely covered by a picture of Ha Long Bay, he set up their table and chairs near the top of a cliff where they watched the sun set over the ocean. The beach had been such a big part of their life. It was wrong that it now represented tragedy rather than joy. Sophie hadn't been back to the beach since. She couldn't imagine doing it just yet. The same way she couldn't ever imagine having a date night again.

Finally settling on which dress to wear, she pulled it over her head then went into the bathroom to put on some makeup. Not a lot. She was someone who never wore much anyway, but as Jess was going to the trouble of cooking her dinner, she figured she could at least put on lipstick and mascara as well as dab perfume on her wrists.

Standing in front of the mirror, staring at herself, it sunk in for the first time how different she looked. Even with the more nutritious meals she'd preparing for herself lately, she was still underweight. Her face looked tired too, even though she'd been sleeping better. Her hazel eyes didn't have the same sparkle they used to; her hair colour could use a refresh as well. It didn't have the same shine that it used to. She hadn't noticed a hairdresser in town, but there must be one. She'd ask Jess later that evening.

Her reflection was enough for her to realise that she needed to start taking better care of herself. To stop just existing and take steps, no matter how small, to start living again.

'Welcome,' Jess said with a smile on her face.

As Sophie walked in, she was glad she'd made the effort to put on a dress. Jess had done the same, a cobalt, sleeveless shift that showed off her slim and toned figure. It also complemented her long red hair and blue eyes.

'Thank you again for inviting me.'

'I've been looking forward to this all day. I haven't had a girls' night for ages. Mike has taken Aaron to football training, so they'll be gone for a while.'

Sophie smiled. 'A girls' night?'

Jess laughed. 'You know what I mean. I wasn't suggesting we go out partying.'

'I can't remember the last time I went out partying,' Sophie said, laughing as well.

Jess shook her head. 'Me neither. Not that we ever did much partying around here. The only time we did something that could loosely be considered partying was when we used to take an esky full of drinks to someone's property and sit around a bonfire.'

Sophie had never taken an esky full of drinks to a bonfire. When she was younger it was all about nightclubs and Sunday sessions at local pubs listening to live music. Being so young and carefree, it seemed so foreign to her now. She could barely remember the time when life had seemed simple and it was all about having fun. That time was long gone, replaced by something she didn't like.

'Something smells delicious,' Sophie said as she followed Jess into the kitchen, focusing on something other than her thoughts.

'I've made a lamb and rosemary pie.'

'That sounds amazing. Can't wait to try it.'

'Everything sounds amazing when you get to share it with someone,' Jess said as she closed the oven door. 'Just needs a few more minutes.'

As soon as Jess uttered those words about sharing, Sophie felt the tears. Tim always used to say that food tasted better when it was shared with someone.

'What's wrong?' Jess said, putting her arm around Sophie.

It took her a few moments to compose herself before Sophie could answer. When she could, she told Jess about Tim. Catherine and Bev already knew, so there was no point lying about why she was upset.

'That's terrible,' she said when Sophie had finished. 'You poor thing. I can't believe you've been going through this on your own.'

'It's not something I'm going to add to the noticeboard in the town hall.'

'Does anyone else know?'

Sophie nodded and told her about the conversation in the store.

'Well, that's three of us who can be there for you.'

Sophie smiled and thanked Jess, but inside, she wasn't sure. Other people had tried to be there for her ever since it happened, but no one knew what it was like. The pain, the grief, the days she didn't want to get out of bed. And the reminders. They were constant. As much as people had tried, they couldn't help. She was alone.

Over dinner, Sophie asked Jess what it was like growing up in Hillford.

'I loved it, but then again, I don't have anything to compare it to. I've never lived anywhere else.'

'What sort of things did you do when you were growing up?'

'There wasn't a lot to do in town back then,' Jess replied, before pausing and laughing. 'There's still not a lot to do now. But we're used to it.'

Sophie wondered how much the town had changed since Jess was a child. Based on what she'd seen, she guessed it hadn't changed much.

'My friend's and I would take turns going to each other's farms and explore. We'd go to the furthest property boundaries, walking through the bush looking for animals. Or we'd swim in the creeks when they had water in them. We had so much fun and loved every minute of it. I'm sure it was different to what you did.'

Sophie thought about the shops and the movies and the weekend trips to the beach, all of which she shared with Jess.

'Like you, I loved it, but I don't have anything to compare it to.'

Sophie thought about being wrapped up in the life you had and not knowing any different unless something happened that took that life away.

'How long have you known Mike?' Sophie said, pushing that thought away, although she knew it wouldn't stay away long.

'Since high school. But we don't have to talk about that.'

Sophie smiled at Jess' thoughtfulness.

'That's ok. I'm interested.'

'Are you sure it won't upset you?'

It probably will, Sophie thought to herself. But she wanted to get to know Jess better, and she had to learn to deal with things that upset her. So, she nodded.

'We've known each other our whole lives and have been together since grade twelve.'

Sophie nodded. 'I guess everyone here has known each other their whole lives.'

Jess laughed. 'Yes, we have. It's hard to keep anything to yourself.'

Sophie wondered how long it would take the rest of the town to find out about the reason she needed a life change.

'My parents and Mike's parents are good friends, so we spent a lot of time at each other's houses growing up. Our parents were very happy when we got married.'

As she listened to Jess, the memory of meeting Tim came back vividly in her mind. They'd met at an art show. Sophie hadn't been to one before, but a friend of hers had wanted to go, so Sophie tagged along, more to keep her friend company than anything else. But she'd been surprised by how much she'd enjoyed it. It was a small show featuring five local artists, one of whom was Tim, a part-time artist who wanted to be a full-time artist, only it didn't pay enough. She asked him about one of his paintings, and they kept talking, finding one subject after another, only pausing when someone interrupted them. When it was time to go, she said goodbye and started to walk away. Then he came after her and asked her out. She found out later that he'd never done anything like that before. He wasn't usually that bold. But Sophie was glad that on that occasion he had been.

They'd met for dinner the following Friday. Tim had picked a restaurant along the river that had a great view of the bridge and all the boats gliding back and forth. They'd stayed for hours, long after they finished eating, until the staff began to close the restaurant. On Sunday they met for lunch, which turned into an afternoon walk along the beach. Before long they were spending several nights a week in each other's company. Six months later they moved in together. That was five and a half years ago. Six years together in total. It wasn't long enough. Sixty years wouldn't have enough.

'Have you got room for dessert?' Jess queried, interrupting Sophie's thoughts. Something she was pleased about.

'If it's something you made, then definitely,' Sophie said with a smile, although it had taken some effort to plaster the smile in place.

'I made a sticky date pudding. I haven't had one in ages.'

Sophie watched Jess get up and go to the kitchen, after being told that she wasn't to help clean up the dinner plates or serve dessert, even though she'd offered. While Jess was gone, Sophie got up and wandered from the dining room into the living room. From what she'd seen of Jess' house, it matched her personality perfectly. Bright, sunny colours, nothing cluttered, and it had the feeling of being a place you could make yourself at home in without having to worry that you'd forgotten to take your shoes off at the door or put a coffee cup down without a coaster. The house felt warm and inviting, and Sophie hoped she'd come back again. It was so different to where she was living. Yes, the house was light and airy, with no clutter, and she thought her furniture suited, but it didn't feel welcoming. Or even lived in. It was somewhere she slept and bathed, but there were no personal touches. Nothing that gave away anything about who Sophie was or where she'd come from. No photos, no pictures on the walls, no books on the bookshelf. She had those things; she just hadn't taken them out of boxes yet. One day she might. Unless she wasn't in Hillford long enough. The only items she'd added to make the house a bit more homely were the throw cushions on the lounge chairs. They matched perfectly, picked out with Tim when they'd bought the new lounge suite. Every time she plumped one of them up before sitting down, she remembered the day they'd bought them. But they made the lounge chair so comfortable and cosy that she tried not to focus on the memories.

Here at Jess', there was a sideboard against the front wall of the lounge room, underneath the window, and Sophie walked over. It looked like silky oak and an antique, she decided. On top was a collection of photos, all of them either Jess' or

Mike's family members over the years. Some were in black and white, and from the outfits they were wearing, looked to have been taken early last century. Others suggested having been taken in the 1930s and the 1960s. Sophie was intrigued by the people in the photos, wondering what their stories were and what sort of life they lived. Then she came to a row of photos featuring Jess, Mike, and Aaron. In every one of the photos, they looked happy, smiling at the camera that was capturing the moment. Sophie picked one up and stared at it. It was the sort of photo she'd thought she'd have one day. Now she doubted she ever would.

'That was taken on holiday last year,' Jess revealed, as she came out from the kitchen. 'We went to Sydney. Mike wanted to see the Opera House and the Harbour Bridge. Aaron wanted to go to Taronga Zoo.'

'I hope you don't mind me looking at the photos. The lounge room is so inviting, and I went to have a closer look.'

'Of course not. You're welcome to go anywhere. I invited you to all of our house, not just one part of it,' Jess said with a smile.

'Had you been to Sydney before?'

Jess shook her head. 'First time for all of us. What about you?'

'Once, when I was much younger.'

Sophie left out the part where she and Tim had started planning a trip to see the New Year's Eve fireworks. Instead, she told Jess how delicious dessert smelled.

'Time to stop smelling it then and start eating it.'

As they ate, Sophie asked about every ingredient Jess had used. As good as she was at cooking, she'd never been a baker. It had always been in the back of her mind to try, but she'd never got around to it. There were plenty of recipe books in one the boxes she had yet to unpack, recipe books that she hadn't even looked at in years because sweets were never what she created in the kitchen. Boxes that would be staying in one of the spare rooms for the foreseeable future.

On the drive back, Sophie thought about how much she'd enjoyed the night. Yes, there were times when she felt sad, especially when she'd told Jess about Tim. But overall, she'd been relaxed and comfortable in Jess' home. It had been a while since she'd felt that way in anyone's home, even her own. And Jess had given her the details of the local hairdresser who worked from her spare garage, a space she'd fitted out specifically to see clients, explaining why Sophie hadn't noticed a salon in the centre of town. First thing in the morning, she would call and make an appointment. It was a small thing, but a good thing. Something for herself.

The only detail she hadn't been comfortable with that night was returning the favour and inviting Jess over for dinner. Jess hadn't mentioned anything, but Sophie knew she should have. What stopped her was not being ready to cook for anyone else yet. Or unpack her cookbooks. The ones she and Tim used to buy each other when they came across one they thought the other would like.

She'd have to say something the next time she saw Jess. Sophie felt like she'd made a good friend, and she needed to start acting like it. Being alone wasn't something Sophie would ever recommend, and while she wasn't ready for a partner in her life, now or in the future, she was ready for a friend.

Chapter Six

Sophie picked up the book from the top of the pile, turning it over slowly in her hands and reading the back cover. When she'd first suggested a book club, she thought it was a good idea because it would give her something to do. Something to take her mind off her ever-present reality. Now, as she stared down at the book, she wasn't as sure as she'd initially been. She hadn't started reading again or unpacked any of the books still in boxes; the bookcase remained empty in the corner of the lounge room.

A book club signified that not only would she need to start reading again, but she'd also have to finish the book and make notes that she could discuss with others in the meeting. The only person she'd discussed a book she was reading with was Tim. He'd liked hearing her thoughts about the plot, the characters, what she got out of the story. It was the reason she hadn't opened a book for herself, even though she was surrounded by them every day and talked to the customers about their purchases and what they thought of worlds they escaped to in amongst the pages. But those conversations were about their thoughts, not her own, and when she'd been asked for recommendations, that was work, and more about understanding what the customer might like, rather than what she would like. Sophie missed talking to Tim about what she'd read. It was one of a very long list of things she missed. It was a small thing, but it had meant something to her.

She stared at the book for several minutes, her mind tossing between moving ahead with the idea and letting it go all together.

But the book continued to hold her attention, and eventually, she understood that if she was ever going to feel like herself again, she needed to get back to the things she used to enjoy, things she'd gotten pleasure from. There were very few things she found pleasure in right now, and it would be nice to have something.

'You look deep in thought,' Ryan said as he approached the counter.

Sophie's head jerked up, startled. She hadn't heard the door open, and she wasn't expecting anyone except Catherine, who would be there any minute. She'd only arrived ten minutes ago herself, and the store didn't officially open for another twenty minutes, although Catherine never paid much notice to the opening and closing times. If she was there and someone wanted to come in, she let them, something Sophie had started doing as well.

She stared for a moment before remembering that Ryan had texted her two and a half hours ago, saying he would be in town later in the morning and needed to check something about the repairs with her. It was the first time Sophie had seen him in the store. It was also the first time someone had texted her that early. The sun hadn't even risen, and she'd still been in bed,

Molly snuggled in beside her. He must be an early riser, she thought, and probably not the only one considering this was a farming community. Early to bed and early to rise, the opposite of her old life in the city.

'Is that interesting?' he asked, pointing to the book she was still holding.

Sophie shrugged. 'I haven't read this one, so I'm not sure. I wasn't pondering this novel though. I was contemplating one that might be suitable for a book club.'

'I didn't know there was a book club in town.'

Sophie shook her head. 'There isn't yet, but I'm hoping there will be. I talked to Catherine about it, and she thinks it's great idea. I just need to get a few more people involved, and off we go.'

Ryan smiled. 'Between the bookstore and trying to get that up and running, you're becoming part of this town.'

'I guess I am,' Sophie said, although she didn't quite feel that way. Yes, she was meeting people and becoming involved in things, but Hillford still didn't feel like home.

Not wanting the conversation to continue in the same vein, she asked Ryan if he read. And in response, he shook his head.

'Never really been my thing.'

'Maybe you just haven't found the right book.'

Ryan shook his head again. 'I'll leave the reading up to you, but I hope you get the book club up and running.'

Sophie smiled and said thank you. He genuinely seemed to mean it.

'Now, the reason I came in,' he said, reaching into the bag he was carrying. 'I've got the taps for the bathroom sink to show you. These three were left over from previous jobs. If you like one of them, I'll replace the existing tap with that. If not, the hardware store has a few more options. Thought I'd check with you first though. There's no point spending more money if we don't have to.'

It wasn't Sophie's money, but it was nice of him to think of the Andersons, even though when she'd let them know that Ryan was doing the repairs, they hadn't given any indication of a budget they'd like to stick to.

Sophie looked at the three taps he'd put on the counter. The one in the middle was nice. If it had been her house and not someone else's she still would have chosen it.

'Great,' he said. 'I'll fit this the next time I'm over. Should be in a few days.'

Just as he was leaving, he paused for a moment and looked back at her. 'Did you do something with your hair?'

Sophie smiled. 'If you mean did I get a haircut and the colour refreshed, then yes, I did.'

Ryan nodded. 'It suits you.'

Then he turned and headed out the door.

Later that day, her thoughts turned back to the conversation with Ryan and what he said about her getting the book club up and running. It was enough for Sophie to lose the last of the doubts she had, and she began the task of getting members.

Over the next few days, she started off by asking those she already knew - Bev and Maggie, as well as Jess who was becoming a closer friend as the days passed. Jess then asked Pam, one of the other teachers. Sophie was pleased when they all said yes straight away. Adding herself and Catherine, it was enough people to make a start, and they all agreed on the date for the first meeting.

When the night of the first book club arrived, Sophie was delighted that not only was everyone there, but they'd all read the book from first to last page and made notes of things they wanted to talk about.

Sophie had done some research about which novels were well suited to book clubs and put together a list to choose from. She picked the first one from the middle of the list, *The Guernsey Literary and Potato Peel Pie Society* by Mary Ann Shaffer, to get them started. No one in the room had read it, and she'd found lots of discussion topics during her research, just in case she needed some points to get everyone talking.

Catherine had pulled the chairs and tables together, so they were all sitting in a group. Bev had made a frittata and savoury scrolls, which she sliced into bite size pieces and put on a platter in the centre of the table. Jess brought homemade caramel slices and chocolate profiteroles. Maggie brought two bottles of white wine, and Pam had brought two bottles of red wine, all different varietals so the ladies had a choice.

Sophie was looking forward to getting to know Pam. She was the only one in the room that she knew very little about, having only met her once before. She was one of the three teachers at the school and had been there the longest, for almost forty years.

Soon to be two if what Catherine said about Pam wanting to retire was correct, and Sophie assumed it was. There didn't seem to be anything that happened in Hillford that Catherine didn't know about. Some of those things she was willing to share. Others she wasn't. Catherine was a person you could trust, and she wouldn't share anything unless she knew it was ok to do so.

When everyone was seated, Sophie addressed the group. 'Thank you so much for coming. When I initially thought about starting a book club here, I wasn't sure if anyone would be interested. Or if people would say they were, then not turn up. But you all did, and I'm really looking forward to this. I hope you are too.'

Around the room, heads nodded.

Bev spoke first. 'We all spend so much time wrapped up in our lives—running farms, running shops, teaching children. It will be nice to use our brains in a different way.'

Maggie agreed, a smile spreading across her face. 'And it will be nice to read something that doesn't involve the amount that I owe for everything I order. Or how many bottles of milk are arriving on a Monday morning.'

The others laughed, and Sophie took the opportunity to look more closely at Pam. There was a sparkle in her brown eyes, ones that were almost the same colour as her hair, courtesy of a bottle now, Sophie guessed. She wasn't a tall woman, which made her curvy figure look even curvier. If Sophie had to describe how she looked, jovial is the word she'd use.

'I know what you mean,' Jess said. 'As much as I love teaching, it will be nice to read something for myself and not something I have to mark.'

Pam nodded in agreement. 'Couldn't agree more, Jess, especially as the books we read are likely to be well written and feature correct punctuation and grammar, unlike some of the assignments we get.'

The others laughed again.

'I'm glad you suggested it and that we're all here,' Pam continued. 'I love to read, and it will be so nice to talk to others about what I've read. I have all sorts of thoughts running through my head about a book when I've finished it. Especially ones that I like.'

Everyone turned to look at Catherine, but she just smiled and said that everyone else had covered what she was going to say.

Sophie picked up the book. 'Let's get started then. I wrote down some questions we can use if we need them. Or we can just start by saying what we thought of the book.'

'I loved it,' Jess said. 'Is that a good starting point?'

Sophie smiled. 'Absolutely. What did you love the most about it?'

'The spirit of those characters who had to tolerate terrible hardships during the German occupation and how they kept going, looked after each other, and were there for each other.'

Pam nodded. 'I liked that too. And the book had such a lovely feel about it too. Heart-warming is probably how I would describe it.'

'It reminded me that, with people around you, most things can be overcome,' Maggie said. 'Much like this town. We've always been there for each other.'

Catherine nodded. 'We're not an island, but we are a community.'

Sophie gazed around the room, the other participants smiling at each other. Would she ever feel like she was an integral part of that community?

'What did everyone think of the book being composed of letters?' Sophie asked, changing the focus of her thoughts. 'Did that make it hard to read for anyone? Or was it easy?'

'I found it hard at first,' Jess said. 'But then I got used to it.'

Maggie nodded. 'Same for me. It took a couple of chapters, but then I didn't notice anymore.'

'I liked it,' Pam said. 'It reminded me of the letters I used to write as a child to my pen pals.'

Sophie was intrigued. 'I've never had a pen pal. What did you write about?'

'Anything and everything,' Pam replied. 'School, friends, family, what I did on weekends or the holidays. I'd ask lots of questions too, so I could find out more about their lives and what they were doing.'

'How did you meet your pen pals?' Sophie asked, still fascinated by the idea.

'I had three, and I met each of them on holidays,' Pam said. 'We used to spend two weeks on the Gold Coast just after Christmas. Their families did the same, so we got to spend that time together. The rest of the year, we wrote to each other.'

'Have you always lived in Hillford, Pam?' Sophie enquired.

Pam shook her head. 'I moved here after graduating from teachers' college. I won't tell you how many years ago that was, but you can probably guess.'

Jess smiled. 'I think the name teachers' college gives it away.'

Pam laughed. 'I guess it does. Unlike you, we didn't have to go to university back then.'

'What made you choose this town?' Sophie said.

'When I graduated, I needed to do what was called rural service, which was ok with me as I grew up a few hours north of here in a town around the same size, so I was used to rural living. This job came up, I applied, and I got it.'

Catherine smiled. 'I can't imagine there were too many people who wanted to move somewhere remote like this.'

Pam smiled too, then shook her head. 'No, it was always hard to get teachers out this way, or anywhere in the west or the far north of the state. Hasn't changed much since then either. It's still hard to get people to come out here. That's why it's nice that you've come. It's good to have some new faces in town.'

Sophie listened to Pam's words and added another person to her list of people who were happy she was here. So far, the list was ninety nine percent in the positive column. It was only Harry who was in the negative. But she was also aware that Pam's words had opened the way for questions to be asked about how she came to be in Hillford, and she didn't want to talk about any of that with those that didn't know yet. Instead, she continued with her questions for Pam.

'You've never thought of going anywhere else? Or going back to the town you grew up in?'

Pam shook her head. 'There was nothing to go back to. My parents couldn't understand why I wanted a career. It wasn't something many women did back then. I was supposed to marry a farmer, have children, spend my life looking after them, and any time that was left over was for doing the household chores. That was never a life I wanted.'

Bev nodded. 'And it's one you've never given in to pressure to conform to. I admire you're spirit and your conviction.'

'I'll admit that there have been times when I've been lonely, but overall, I like being by myself, and I'm very happy with the life I've lived and continue to live. This is my home. I tried city life once, and I found it wasn't for me, so I came back and never left again.'

Then Pam turned towards Bev. 'And if there's anyone else I know who isn't one to give in to pressure, it's you.'

Everyone in the room laughed, even Sophie who knew enough about Bev by now to know that was true. She can't imagine Bev ever doing anything she didn't want to.

'Anyway, that's enough about me,' Pam said. 'What were we talking about?'

'Pen pals,' Maggie said. 'That's brought back some memories.'

Catherine nodded. 'For me too.'

Maggie turned to Catherine. 'Do you remember running to the letterbox and finding a letter? It was such a thrill. It might seem foreign to those of you who are younger, but when we were growing up, there was no other way to connect with people outside of Hillford. It was too expensive to make long distance phone calls, so relying on the post is what we did.'

Catherine nodded. 'We rarely made long distance phone calls back then. And yes, I do remember running to the letterbox when I got home from school. I haven't thought about the letters I received from my pen pals for years. It's a nice memory.'

'Did you have any pen pals, Bev?' Sophie asked.

'Sort of. I didn't have any that were specifically pen pals, but I had several cousins in different parts of the state, and we used to write to each other. I loved getting those letters.'

Sophie's thoughts were taken back to the city, more specifically, the notes Tim would leave for her. Often simple ones, like leaving a note under her handbag saying that he hoped she had a good day at the library, or a note in her lunch bag about enjoying the food he'd prepared for her to take to work. Sometimes he would leave notes in drawers he knew she opened on regular occasions, telling her how much he loved her. She still had them all, tied together with a ribbon in the unopened box with the other mementos of their time together. But now was not the time to think about those. It was time to get back to discussing the book.

'As the story was set during World War II, was there anything in particular that stood out about that time in history and the events that occurred?' Sophie asked.

'For me, it was the time period in general,' Catherine said. 'More so because I remember my parents telling me what it was like during those years. They were London born and bred, and up until the day they both died, they remember what it was like during the Blitz, almost as if it had ended only days before. After everything they went through during the war years, they eventually decided they wanted a new life, so the three of us emigrated.'

Jess turned to look at Catherine. 'I didn't know you were from London, and I've known you all my life.'

'I probably never mentioned it. I was only two years old when we moved to Australia back in 1954, so I don't think of myself as being from London.'

'There's a tie-in with the book,' Maggie said. 'Juliet is from London.'

Catherine nodded and smiled. 'Yes, that thought did cross my mind. Not for long though. I was too busy thinking about my parents and the things they talked about.'

'Never having lived through anything like that,' Sophie said. 'I can't imagine what it was like.'

Catherine nodded again. 'I can't either. Even though I heard the stories, I never lived them. But for those that did, it was an awful time.'

Maggie looked at the others in the room. 'Is it wrong to be thankful that we've never had to go through anything like that?'

Bev shook her head. 'No, but I don't think there's anyone in this room who hasn't gone through hard times, ones they'd wished they hadn't. As long as we don't forget what others have gone through, just as the characters didn't. Even though it's fiction, I can't help thinking the feelings are real. Just like the feelings we've all had at certain times.'

Sophie had the same thoughts while she'd been reading. But she didn't want any more feelings filling her mind that night. So, she steered the conversation back by using the prompts she'd found until everyone had said all they intended to.

'We don't have to use the books on the list,' Sophie declared after the conversation stopped. 'They're just some suggestions. If anyone has a book they'd like to discuss at the next book club, now is the time to mention it.'

'I can't think of any off the top of my head so I'm happy to go with one from the list,' Bev stated. 'What about everyone else?'

Around the room, the others nodded in agreement.

Sophie pulled out the list she'd written and picked one at random. 'In that case, the next book is *The Light Between Oceans* by ML Steadman. Has anyone read it?'

Everyone's head shook in unison.

'Ok, I'll order some copies tomorrow. They should be here in a few days, which will give everyone time to finish it before the next meeting.'

'Looking forward to it,' Bev said.

Jess nodded as she put that meeting's book in her handbag. 'That was great. I really enjoyed tonight.'

Pam nodded. 'So did I.'

Sophie smiled. 'It wouldn't have been the success it was without the effort you all put in.'

'I've missed being in a book club,' Pam said. 'I was in one years ago, during that brief time I mentioned earlier, when I moved to the city with my friend Elise.'

'That is going back a long way,' Bev said.

'Are you reminding me that I'm old?' Pam said, but with a smile.

Bev laughed. 'If you're old, then so am I. We're the same age, remember?'

'Elise,' Maggie said. 'There's someone I haven't seen for a long time.'

'Who's Elise?' Sophie asked, not recalling hearing that name since she'd arrived.

'Ryan's mum,' Pam replied. 'She and I moved to the city when we were in our early thirties. I came back after six months, but Elise stayed.'

'So how did Ryan end up here if he was brought up in the city, which I assume he was if that's where his mum lived,' Sophie asked.

Pam nodded. 'Yes, he was brought up in the city, but when he was child, Elise would bring him back for holidays to visit her parents. He told me he moved back here because he always preferred it to the city.'

'That's not what I heard,' Bev said.

Pam turned to look at her. 'What did you hear?'

'Maybe we should leave that for now,' Catherine said, changing the course of the conversation. 'Ryan probably wouldn't like us talking about him.'

'You're right,' Bev said. 'Let's leave it there.'

While the conversation continued around her, Sophie couldn't help but wonder what Bev had heard. She also wondered why she was so interested in knowing the answer. But the thought didn't stay long as she saw Jess starting to gather the rest of her things.

'I just wanted to thank you again for inviting me over for dinner. I had a wonderful time.'

Jess smiled. 'I'm glad you enjoyed it.'

'I'd like to return the favour. It's just that I haven't cooked for anyone else since Tim passed away. It's something we enjoyed doing together. and I don't feel ready just yet. I hope you don't mind.'

Jess shook her head. 'Of course not. Whenever you're ready, let me know.'

As everyone stood up to go, Sophie reminded them she'd put the order in tomorrow morning and would let them know when the books arrived. After goodbyes and several hugs, the only people left in the bookstore were Sophie and Catherine.

Catherine turned to look at Sophie. 'That was a great night. I'm glad you suggested starting this. It will be good for everyone. Especially you.'

As she drove home, Sophie thought about what Catherine had said. And realised she was right.

Chapter Seven

Sophie made the coffee in silence. Even though things had been cordial between herself and Harry, and they'd been conversing from time to time, it seemed this morning wasn't going to be one of those occasions. Harry had walked in and grunted in the direction of the coffee machine. Sophie had almost made up her mind to ignore him, but something stopped her. There was a look on his face that she hadn't seen before. And for some reason, it bothered her. Considering his behaviour to date, it shouldn't have. But Sophie felt like something wasn't right.

'Your coffee is almost ready, Harry.'

When he didn't respond, Sophie tried again.

'Do you want anything to go with it? A muffin or a slice?'

For a second time, he didn't answer. Instead, he was staring at a photo book that Sophie had put on display the day before, featuring images from beaches around the world. When Sophie ordered it, she doubted anyone in town would want to buy it. And she'd had second thoughts herself, given how close to a beach Tim had been when he lost his life. But she'd been missing the beach recently, even with the negative thoughts that came with it, and if she couldn't get to one, at least she could look at pictures. She was about to call Harry out for ignoring her when she noticed he had tears in his eyes.

Sophie hesitated for a moment. She wasn't sure how Harry would react if he knew she'd noticed. But she couldn't ignore what was right in front of her.

'Are you all right, Harry?'

He turned away and Sophie saw him wipe his eyes.

'Is my coffee ready?'

Sophie picked up the cup and took it over to him. And asked him if he was ok.

'Yes, yes. Just memories.'

'Something the book reminded you of?'

Harry nodded but didn't say anything. The tears were gone, but the sadness was still in his eyes.

'Do you want to sit down for a moment?'

Harry seemed to be thinking about it, and Sophie wasn't sure what he would do. But then he sat down. So, she sat down with him.

He looked at the book cover one more time then turned towards Sophie.

'Everyone else in town knows, so you may as well.'

Harry paused for a moment, took a sip of coffee and then continued.

'It's about my wife and son.'

Now it was Sophie's turn to pause. In the time since she'd been in town, she hadn't heard any mention of Harry being married or being a father.

'It was a long time ago now. We went to the beach for a holiday. They got caught in a rip. And they drowned.'

'Oh, Harry. I'm so sorry.'

He nodded to acknowledge what she said. 'I've never been back to the beach.'

Sophie nodded. 'I can understand why. The reminders. The pain and the grief.'

Harry looked up and stared at directly at her face, his eyes narrowing. 'What do you know about grief?'

And so, she told him about Tim. It surprised her because that was a topic she never thought she'd talk about with Harry. Not based on how they'd got along so far. But learning about Harry's tragedy changed things. And gave her an insight into why he was the way he was.

'Something we share then,' Harry said, his face still covered by a veil of sadness. 'It's a terrible thing to have in common though.'

Sophie nodded. 'It is. It's not something I would wish on anyone.'

Harry nodded in agreement.

'What was it like, being in a small town, where I assume everyone knew?'

For Sophie, only her family and friends knew. The rest of the city carried on, unaware and uncaring about her loss.

Harry thought for a moment before speaking.

'I've lived in this town my whole life, so I know almost everyone, and I count many of them as friends. But after Emma and Patrick passed away, those same people fell into two groups. The first didn't know what to say and so avoided me. The second wouldn't leave me alone, constantly checking on me as if I'd suddenly become helpless and unable to feed, bathe, and clothe myself.'

As Harry was speaking, memories flashed through Sophie's mind. Memories of awkward encounters with friends who also didn't know what to say. Constant messages from others checking if she was ok, when one message would have done. Invitations to various outings from those who'd never had to deal with a grief like the one that had consumed Sophie because they thought she wanted to be occupied when all she wanted was to be left alone.

'Depending on the day, one was easier to manage than the other,' Harry said.

Sophie nodded, his words continuing to ring true in her ears.

'There were days where I bumped into those who didn't know what to say, and I let it wash over me. Then on other days, I wanted to say something, ask them why they couldn't find a few words. I never did though.'

Sophie nodded again, having experienced the same thoughts Harry was describing.

'And then there were days I would hear a knock on the door, and I would debate whether or not to open it. If I didn't, I'd come out later and usually find a dish with a casserole or some other meal in it.'

Sophie smiled.

'What are you smiling for? I got very annoyed at that. Did people think I couldn't look after myself?'

'I doubt that's why people left you meals. I think it's more likely that they wanted to do something for you and weren't sure what else to do. At least leaving a meal was practical.'

Harry looked sceptical for a moment but then shrugged. 'I guess so. Did you get casseroles?'

'Yes, and I was grateful for them.'

'Why? I'm sure you can cook.'

'I can, but cooking was something Tim and I used to do together. We'd go out on a weekend and buy the ingredients we needed for the week. We'd go to markets and delis and tiny grocery stores that we found which specialised in hard-to-get items. Then each night we'd cook together while we told each other about our days and listened to music. After he passed away, I didn't want to go into the kitchen at all.'

'Do you cook now?'

'I do, but just basic things so I have something to eat for dinner. The recipe books we used are still in a box.'

'Maybe you should get them out again.'

'Have you gone back to anything that reminds you of Emma and Patrick?'

Harry gave her a look which clearly expressed that she shouldn't have asked that question. But later, after he left, she thought about what he'd said about the recipe books. She wasn't ready to pull them out yet, and she wasn't sure when she would be. But at some point, she'd like to prepare some of the meals outlined on the pages again.

At the second book club, a week later, as Sophie watched everyone take their place, she glanced at the book in her hands, and her conversation with Harry came back to her.

Of all the books to pick she thought, given what he'd told her. *The Light Between Oceans* by ML Steadman. Not the same story, but the word ocean in the title was enough for her to remember the sadness in his voice, the same sadness that shrouded his face. The same sadness that mirrored her own.

'Is everyone ready to get started?' Sophie asked, pushing the thoughts in her head to the side.

Around the room, everyone nodded.

'Who'd like to start?

'I will,' Bev said. 'I was surprised by this book. From the blurb on the back, I thought it wouldn't be my sort of book. But I found I quite enjoyed it. Maybe it's the location, so far from anything. Reminded me a bit of being in a town like this, so far away from the wider world.'

Pam nodded in agreement. 'Yes, we are quite isolated, but that's why we're all here. We don't want to be surrounded by hustle and bustle.'

Hustle and bustle are what Sophie had been used to her whole life. Now though, there were moments, more and more of them, where she appreciated the quieter, slower pace.

'I liked that it was by an Australian author,' Pam continued. 'There were plenty of things I identified with. Most books you read are by overseas authors, and it's hard to relate sometimes.'

Maggie nodded. 'I agree. It's so nice to read something that's Australian.'

'I know,' Jess chimed in. 'We have so many creative, talented people in this country who are often ignored by the rest of the world.'

Sophie smiled. 'All great points. So, Bev, apart from the location, were there other things you enjoyed about the book?'

Bev leaned forward and picked up the book from the table where it had been laying in front of her. 'Yes, but I'd like to expand on the location a bit more first. When I think about a lighthouse, I think of it as a symbol for safety and hope for those sailing on wild, dark seas at night. Seeing the light from the lighthouse reminds you that you're not the only one in the darkness.'

Not being the only one in the darkness was something Sophie had craved for months after Tim's passing. Still craved it now at times.

'I felt the same,' Maggie added. 'Not that I've ever sailed, but just thinking what it would be like on the ocean at night, I like the idea that the lighthouse is a beacon of hope.'

'The other main point for me,' Bev said, flicking through the pages, 'was the moral dilemma. It wasn't her baby, but she kept the child anyway.'

Catherine concurred. 'It's a moral dilemma, but one I can't imagine many people would ever have to face. Even though I don't condone the actions she took, it's one of the main points of the story, and it wouldn't be the same novel without that part of the plot.'

Jess put down the copy she was holding. 'I can see from the way the author explained it why she did what she did and how it was central to the story, but after that, I found it hard to keep reading. No matter what was going on in her life, what she did was unforgiveable.'

'I think you're able to bring a different perspective to the book because of the age of your son,' Pam said. 'It's been a long time since any of our children were babies. Aaron is only eight. Your baby years are still recent. Having said that, I can't excuse her actions either. I couldn't imagine what it would be like if it was my baby that had been taken. And it's not something I could ever do, no matter what the circumstances were.'

Sophie stopped the discussion. 'I thought you never married, Pam?'

Pam shook her head. 'I didn't. But that doesn't mean I didn't have a child.'

The look of confusion on Sophie's face was enough to keep Pam talking.

'Yes, even back then, when it wasn't convention, I knew I wanted a child. I just didn't want a husband.'

Sophie looked at Pam with newfound admiration. Given Pam's age, it must have been very difficult to be a single mother at the time her baby had been born.

'I didn't know that. Tell me about her, or him.'

'Her. Cara. She's an accountant. Works for a big, multi-national firm in the city. She's married and has given me three adorable grandchildren.'

'Does she know her...' Sophie stopped herself before asking the rest of the question. 'Apologies Pam, I shouldn't be asking such personal questions.'

Pam smiled. 'That's ok. Everyone else in town knows the story. And yes, she does know her father. They have a very good relationship. I have a good relationship with him too. We're friends, have been since we were children. But neither of us wanted to follow the traditional path, so we made our own. Cara spent time with both of us growing up. With me more so when she was younger, but as she got older, her time was split equally between us.'

Sophie processed what she'd just heard. Admittedly she didn't know Pam that well, but there'd been no indication, at least not in front of Sophie, that she'd done something so courageous, ignoring society's standards and probably losing friends and possibly family along the way. Turns out that wasn't the case at all.

'I'll introduce you the next time Cara is in town. But for now, we should probably get back to the book because I think a few others want to have a say.'

Pam was smiling as she said it, but she was right. They could talk about her daughter another time. So instead, she turned towards the person who was fast becoming the closest friend Sophie had made since before losing Tim.

'What do you think, Jess, about the comments around the age of everyone's children?'

'Aaron's age probably did give me a different perspective, but even if it hadn't, I think I still would have found it hard to finish it.'

'That's perfectly understandable,' Sophie said. 'Did anyone else have trouble reading it?'

The others shook their heads.

'I was uncomfortable about that part of the story,' Maggie said. 'But I just kept reminding myself that's all it was, a story. Made up.'

Bev nodded. 'Same here. I'd love to know how the author came up with the idea for the story. Or if there were any misgivings about having that storyline.'

'Did anyone else think about what they'd do if they found themselves in the same situation as Isabel, the protagonist Tom's wife?' Sophie asked.

No one spoke, but Sophie could tell that they'd all had, even the ones who'd already stated Isabel's actions are ones they could never replicate.

'Did anyone else notice that like our first book, this one also had a theme about war?' Catherine asked, changing the subject. 'In this case, the First World War, not the second.'

Sophie nodded. 'I didn't think about that though when I suggested it for book club.'

'I couldn't help but feel sorry for him, even though, at the start, he was part of the cover up with the baby,' Catherine said. 'But dealing with nightmares and the guilt of having survived had an impact on who he was.'

Pam nodded. 'And there was no help for anyone back then. Men were just expected to come home and get on with their lives as if nothing had happened. I can understand why the character wanted to live in the middle of the ocean in a lighthouse.'

'Yes, I can too,' Maggie said. 'But there came a point where he got married, and then went along with what his wife chose to do.'

'And then she was angry at him for what she thought was his betrayal, even though he was doing the right thing,' Jess said.

The discussion continued for over an hour, and the whole time, Sophie thought about Harry and what had happened to his family. The book had been very emotional, but as Jess had said earlier, it was only fiction. The emotions Harry had gone through were real. Just like hers.

Had Harry felt guilty? And if so, did he still carry that feeling with him? She wasn't sure it was a question she could ever ask him.

Later that night, after she arrived home, Sophie pulled the boxes that contained her books out of the cupboard where she'd been storing them and unpacked them, placing each one on the previously empty shelves on her bookcase. By the time she'd finished, the bookcase had lost the neglected look that had come from being bare. With her books all in place, the bookcase had a new lease of life. Maybe she wouldn't be too much further behind.

The following morning, as she drove to the bookstore, she saw Ryan driving the other way. He waved when he saw her, and she returned the gesture. It reminded her of what she wanted to ask Catherine.

'You don't have to answer if you don't want to,' Sophie said after she'd posed her questions about why Ryan had come back to town as well as what Bev had said at the first book club.

Catherine paused for a moment before responding. 'Ryan has never been one to share what's going on in his life, but most people guessed the reason he came back. I don't suppose it matters if I tell you. Someone else will eventually.'

Sophie wasn't sure why she wanted to know, but she'd been curious about it ever since the night the topic had come up.

'It's true that Ryan loved spending his holidays here. He was always more of a country boy than a city boy. But then he fell in love, and she had no desire to move to the country. They were together for years until she broke his heart. And then he came back here to heal and start again.'

Healing and starting again was something Sophie was extremely familiar with, and she wondered if it had worked for Ryan. If it did, maybe it would work for her.

'As far as I'm aware, he hasn't been in a relationship since. Doesn't mean he's not interested. Just that he hasn't found the right person yet.'

As she spoke, Catherine didn't take her eyes off Sophie. But even though Sophie knew what was going through Catherine's mind, she also knew that right person wasn't her.

It didn't stop her bringing up the subject with Jess though, when she arrived on Saturday morning for a coffee.

'How well do you know Ryan?' Sophie asked once she'd carried two cups and a plate of biscuits outside to the front verandah.

Molly looked up at her expectantly, but Sophie shook her head. The biscuits were treats for people, not puppies.

'Fairly well, but I could say that about a lot of people in town,' Jess said with a smile.

Sophie laughed. 'I should know that by now, but I keep forgetting that everyone knows everyone else. So different to where I'm from.'

'You'll get used to it. And you'll realise that anything you don't want the whole town knowing about is best kept to yourself.'

Sophie nodded. That was something she'd realised early on and always kept in the back of her mind.

'That's something Ryan is very good at. Keeping things to himself.'

'What do you mean?'

'He doesn't say a lot. Most people only know him on a superficial level, which is his choice. But we grew up together in the years before he moved and then we reconnected when he came back, so he trusts me because he knows me.'

'He doesn't trust many people?'

Jess shook her head. 'It's not surprising given what happened to him.'

Sophie paused for a moment before asking the next question. 'Was it really that bad a break-up?'

'I've never gone through anything like you've experienced, or have a relationship end, so I can't comment on what either situation feels like. All I can say in Ryan's case is that his parent's divorce, which wasn't amicable, held him back from getting close to someone. For years, he had no interest in being in a relationship. He saw firsthand what happens when things go terribly wrong, and he was worried about history repeating itself.'

Sophie's parents were still together, but she could see how parents divorcing, particularly if it was nasty, would make someone cautious about relationships.

'When he finally did make a commitment to someone, it ended badly. I won't share the exact details because I don't think he'd want me to. But he's been on his own ever since, even though almost every single woman in town around his age has shown interest at one time or another.'

Given how handsome Ryan was, Sophie wasn't surprised.

'He's a great guy,' Jess continued. 'He's just put a wall up around himself, one that you seem to be getting through.'

Sophie put her coffee cup down. 'Me? What do you mean?

'You talk with him when he comes over don't you?'

Sophie nodded. 'Of course. Why wouldn't I?'

Jess smiled. 'He does work for a lot of people, and from what I've heard, he doesn't say a lot when he's at their homes. When he comes here, he has a good old chat.'

'I can't imagine that's true. I'm sure he has the same conversations with everyone else. Now, would you like some more biscuits?'

Jess grinned. 'Nice change of subject, but yes, I would. Did you make them?'

Sophie nodded. 'Bev has hinted more than once that at some point, I could contribute to the sweet treats sold at the bookstore.'

Jess laughed. 'I knew that was coming. You'll be baking for the store before you know it.'

Sophie shook her head. 'I don't know about that. The biscuits are my first attempt at baking. They taste ok, but they don't look like they're supposed to.'

'Do you have a biscuit cutter?'

Sophie shook her head again.

'That's the secret to getting them to look like they do in the recipe book pictures. You can buy them in all shapes and sizes.'

'I don't think I'll need any. This is likely to be my first and last attempt.'

Jess laughed. 'You've forgotten how persuasive Bev can be.'

After Jess left, Sophie thought about how unfair life could be. Just in this one, small town alone, she'd already learnt the stories of several people who'd had things happen in their lives that they wished hadn't. As she reflected on the stories she'd heard, sitting on her verandah with Molly at her feet, she had a realisation. What happened to Tim and everything that came after had been terrible. Still was terrible. But she wasn't alone. She wasn't the only one who had gone through a life changing experience. And that gave her hope that one day, she'd come out on the other side of her grief.

Walking back inside, Sophie pulled out the box that contained the special mementos that she'd kept. The letters, photos, cards, and drawings. She only managed to pull a few things out before her emotions took over and she put everything back. It was too soon. But at least she'd made a start. Before now, the box had stayed shut, taped down with the same tape she'd used when she'd packed it back in the city.

One of the things she'd looked at during those few minutes the box was open was the first birthday card Tim had given her. He always took his time with cards, picking out the one he thought was perfect for the occasion and then spending as much time as he needed to make sure the words he wrote conveyed exactly what he wanted them to. Sophie treasured that first card and all the ones that came after. Not just birthdays or anniversaries, but for many other reasons: ones to remind her how important she was to him, ones that said she was always in his thoughts, ones for no other reason than to make her smile. Prior to that, cards she'd received, especially those from the men in her life, had minimal words inscribed, mostly general phrases with no thought to individualising them to her. But Tim's were different. One day, she'd read all of them again. But not today.

The other mementos she'd held in her hands before placing them back in the box were a photo taken at a dinner party they hosted and a drawing Tim had done of the house. As she'd peered at the photo, she couldn't help noticing that everyone in it, herself and Tim as well as their friends, were all laughing. The kind of carefree laughter that represented good times with good friends, and no other thoughts past what they were doing at that moment. As she'd put the photo back, Sophie wondered if she'd ever host a dinner party again. And if she did, would there ever be laughter like that?

As well as being a talented painter, Tim had also been amazing at drawing. The picture, a front view of the house they'd shared, captured not only the building itself, but also the essence of the life they'd lived within its walls. Sitting on the floor in the spare room of the house where she currently lived, there was no soul, no character at all. It was just a building. And it felt stifling. That was the moment she pushed the box back inside the cupboard it had come from and strode outside, needing fresh air and open space.

From the minute she'd got up and Molly heard her footsteps on the timber floor boards, the puppy jumped off its bed and trotted along behind her. Out the front door, down the stairs, and along the driveway. And the sense of comfort the roly-poly bundle gave Sophie was something she was grateful for.

Just before she turned onto the road, she looked back at the house. It was too big for just one person. She tried to imagine what it had been like when it was filled by a family. Maggie had told her there were four Anderson children, so six people had roamed its hallways and resided within its rooms. It would have been a different house then. Full of life, love, and laughter. Very different to what it was now. And it was almost like the house could feel that, like it was waiting to be transformed back into a vibrant residence, bursting at the seams with life. The more Sophie stared, the more she wondered how Tim would have drawn it. He would have captured it perfectly. And if he'd been there to capture it, the house would have been a happy one.

Not just a house, though. A home.

Chapter Eight

When Sophie woke the next morning, she was content to lay in bed for a while, rather than jump up and rush into the day. Until, after a few minutes of snuggling further into the blankets, something Molly adorably replicated, she remembered Ryan telling her he was going to stop by early and get started in the bathroom. That was enough to get her out of bed. One, so she could use that room before it was out of commission, and two, she didn't want Ryan to see her in her pyjamas. Tim had been the only man to see her in pyjamas for a very long time, and she wasn't ready to add another name to the list.

'Morning.'

Sophie heard his voice before she saw him, so she called out in the general direction it came from. 'Would you like a coffee?'

'That'd be great,' Ryan said as he walked into the kitchen a moment later. 'I'll just put the tools in the bathroom and come back for it.'

While he was doing that, Sophie sliced the banana bread that she'd baked the night before and put it in the toaster. Jess had been right. Bev kept mentioning baking sweets for the store, and she knew it was only a matter of time before she gave in, so she figured she'd better practice before bringing in anything people would need to pay for. This was her first attempt at banana bread, and with Ryan in the house, she had a taste tester on hand.

'Something smells good,' he declared as he came back into the room, just as Sophie was buttering the now toasted banana bread.

'Be honest about what it tastes like,' she said, handing him a slice on a plate. 'I'm practising for when the day comes that I'm on the store's baking roster.'

After taking the first bite, he was quiet, and Sophie started to worry. But then she realised it was because he was too busy going for a second bite and then a third. When he'd finished, he asked if there was more.

Sophie smiled. 'I guess I have my answer about how it tastes.'

'It's delicious. I can't believe you haven't made this before. What else do you make?'

'Not much in the sweets department yet. But I'm going to try a few different recipes.'

'Well, I think they'll all be a hit with the customers. I'm sure they'd like anything you do. As I do.'

Sophie suddenly felt flustered and didn't respond. Instead, she just watched as Ryan finished the second slice and then got to work.

After he left the room, Sophie stood still for a few minutes, repeating the same words in her head. He was just talking about the banana bread; he was just talking about the banana bread. There was nothing more to it than that. Then the conversation with Jess came back to her. Surely the friendly tone and easy-going manner Ryan had displayed was on par with how he interacted with other clients.

That thought stayed with her for the rest of the day; from the moment she left for work, to the moment she hopped in her car at 5.30 pm. She'd thought about asking Catherine for her opinion, but something held her back. Catherine knew everything about everybody, and Sophie wasn't ready to hear if she agreed with Jess.

When she got back to the house that afternoon, she was thrilled with what Ryan had done in the bathroom. Not only had he fitted the new the taps, he'd also replaced the cracked tiles and adjusted the height of the mirror so she no longer had to stand on tiptoes to see more than the top half of her face. Plus, he'd fixed the shower head, so the water now came streaming out, rather than the trickle she'd gotten used to.

Walking back to the kitchen, she picked up her phone and sent Ryan a thank you text. He replied within a minute, saying it was his pleasure. This was quickly followed by another text saying he was looking forward to the next time he came back. Sophie stared at the second message, trying to decipher if there was a hidden meaning. Then she shook her head and decided he was just referring to getting the work done so he could get paid and move on to the next job. Surely.

Tired after a busy day and wanting a distraction from thinking about the meaning behind the texts, Sophie picked up the novel that was sitting on the coffee table. It had arrived at the store that morning and was the next one the book club members would be discussing. Even though the participants seemed to be enjoying book club, she still felt, as the instigator and now organiser, she needed to be fully prepared each month. So, she took the paperback, a notebook to write her thoughts in, and Molly's bed out to the verandah. Even though the chill of winter was in the air, Sophie didn't want to be inside, so instead, she settled herself into the rocking chair that the Anderson's had left behind. She'd never owned a rocking chair, and it had taken her a while to get used to it. But now that she had, there was something comforting about it, something reminiscent of a character in a fairy tale. Just not the fairy tale with the big, bad wolf; one of the more pleasant ones.

As she stretched to her left to grab a blanket from the blanket box, also left behind, the last rays of daylight streaked across the landscape. And as she gazed at the sky, enveloped within the woollen folds of the blanket, she felt a moment of peace, the kind of peace she hadn't felt for a long time. She didn't know if it was a result of her surroundings or because she could feel herself beginning to heal. Whatever it was, Sophie didn't want to let it go.

By the time the third book club came around, Sophie's love of reading had fully returned, and other novels, apart from those set for the meetings, had joined her reading pile. This month's book was *Still Alice* by Lisa Genova. She vaguely remembered the movie but had never read the book before it became this month's pick.

'Who'd like to start this time?' she asked, once everyone had taken their place.

'I will,' Pam said. 'Just give me a minute to put my jacket back on. Winter is well and truly here.'

Maggie nodded. 'I put an extra blanket on the bed last night. I'll be glad when spring rolls around.'

Spring, Sophie thought, traditionally a time of new beginnings. A season to grow and flourish. She wondered if that would happen for her.

'I had mixed feelings about this book,' Pam said, jacket firmly in place. 'I liked that it was written about a topic that isn't usually the focus of a story. But then, the thought that something like that could happen to me, that wasn't a nice feeling.'

Sophie nodded. 'It is a scary thought. Was there anyone in your family who had Alzheimer's disease?'

Pam shook her head.

'Anyone else's family?' Sophie asked.

Around the room, everyone shook their heads. Then Catherine and Bev shared a glance. After a moment or two, Catherine spoke.

'Not a family member, but Harry's wife Emma was in the early stages when she died. I don't think he'd mind me saying so. Emma told those she knew about her diagnosis.'

Bev nodded. 'I remember her sharing how scared she was. Her mother had Alzheimer's, and it took her life. Emma had watched it all, so she was terrified by what she knew lay ahead. She didn't want her own life to end that way.'

'But it didn't though, did it?' Jess said, turning to look at the others. 'I thought she drowned.'

Catherine and Bev glanced at each other again, as if deciding what to say next. Then when they turned back to the group, Catherine nodded before speaking.

'She did, but for a long time afterwards, her friends wondered why she'd ever chosen to go to the coast for a holiday in the first place.'

'She never liked swimming, so it seemed like an odd choice,' Bev said. 'We just assumed that Patrick had wanted to go.'

Maggie nodded slowly. 'I remember thinking the same thing.'

'Patrick was in my class,' Pam said, casting her mind back. 'I don't remember him mentioning any desire to head to the seaside.'

'We'll never know why she chose that type of holiday,' Bev disclosed, this time, deliberately not looking in Catherine's direction.

'No, we won't,' Catherine expressed, also avoiding eye contact with Bev. 'How about we go back to the book?'

'Pam, did you want to continue from what you were saying?' Sophie said, bringing the meeting back to topic as Catherine requested.

Pam nodded, picking up her copy of the book. 'There were two main things for me that I couldn't stop thinking about as I read each chapter. The first was her profession, the second was her age.'

Maggie nodded. 'Her age ran through my mind as I read as well. At fifty years old, that's younger than I am now.'

Bev nodded in agreement. 'Apart from Sophie and Jess, we're all older than the character. Alice was older than Emma was though, when she was diagnosed.'

As soon as she'd said it, Bev gazed at Catherine, who shook her head.

'Forget I mentioned anything. We were leaving that topic behind.'

Sophie tried to do what Bev asked but she couldn't. She wanted to know more about Emma. Maybe it would help her understand Harry a little bit better. For all his gruffness, she was developing a soft spot for him.

As she looked around the room, a thought popped into her head. Maybe she could get Harry to come along to book club. She didn't know if he would commit to reading a novel each month, especially ones that weren't of his own choosing, but Sophie was fairly certain he was lonely. A monthly commitment with others might be good for him. She'd just have to think about who else she could invite because she had a feeling Harry wouldn't be comfortable being the only man in the group. She was going through a list of names in her head when Jess jumped in to cover the silence that occurred after Bev spoke.

'Pam, you mentioned her profession. That was something I also contemplated. I know neither of us are Harvard university professors, like Alice was, but we both work in education, and I can't imagine not being able to stand in front of my class teaching them things that, hopefully, sink in.'

At that Pam laughed. 'I've been a teacher a lot longer than you Jess, and you always hope that the knowledge you share registers in their brains. Sometimes it does, other times it doesn't. Certain students I've had over the years, oh my goodness. The stories I could tell. But I won't because they're all adults now and still live in town.'

Jess chuckled. 'I've already had a few of those students.'

Then she turned serious. 'The other thing that affected me as I read was the realisation that the time would come when she wouldn't recognise her children. The thought of not recognising Aaron is heart breaking.'

Again, Sophie's thoughts turned to Emma. How much had she dwelled on that aspect of the disease?

'It does make you think,' Maggie said, interrupting Sophie's train of thought. 'The effect it has on those who love the person with Alzheimer's and the suffering they go through as well. A person who they love with all their heart, but a person who no longer recognises them.'

Catherine nodded. 'That would be an awful place to find yourself in.

'This was such a sad book,' Jess said. 'I hope the next one is cheerful.'

Sophie thought about the book that was next on her list. It was the only one she'd read before, but it was one of her favourites and she wanted to share the enjoyment that she'd gained from the story, enjoyment she hoped the others would share. Now though, it might need a rethink. So, she shook her head and said that it wasn't a chirpy novel, but she would change it if they liked.

'I'm happy not to change it,' Bev said. 'Life is full of ups and downs. It doesn't hurt to be reminded of that.'

Catherine nodded in agreement. 'Let's stick with what you've chosen Sophie, unless anyone has any strong objections.'

Both Maggie and Pam were happy to stick with the choice.

'I am too,' Jess said. 'I just didn't expect this book to affect me so much. But it did and maybe that's a good thing. It got me thinking about what's important. And that's not what I have, but who I have.'

Sophie watched Jess as she spoke. She couldn't have put it better herself. It was who, not what. But the who was gone. Would a time come where she was ready to share her life with someone, in the way she'd done so with Tim?

Later that evening, as she and Catherine packed up, Sophie mentioned the glance and the moment when Catherine shook her head. And how everyone had noticed it.

Catherine sighed. 'I didn't realise it was so obvious.'

'If it's any consolation, it was obvious from Bev too.'

Catherine smiled, although it was only half a smile. 'Bev has never been good at hiding anything. She's always been open and honest and it's one of the things I respect about her.'

Sophie thought about her next words carefully before speaking. 'You think Emma knew she was going into the water that day and not coming out again?'

Catherine nodded. 'I think the realisation of what was going to happen was too much for her.'

'I can't imagine what that must be like.'

'I can't either. Please don't mention this to Harry. As much as he can be a grumpy old man sometimes, he doesn't deserve any more hurt.'

Sophie reached over and squeezed Catherine's hand. 'I won't say anything. Do you think he realises?'

Catherine nodded. 'He'll never say it out loud though. And no one would ever ask him, so we continue to talk about her death as if it was an accident. As for Patrick, that really was just a terrible accident. I don't think Emma realised that Patrick had followed her in. When she started walking out through the waves, Patrick was sitting on the beach with Harry.'

'How did he end up in the water?'

'Harry got up to go to the toilet and told Patrick to stay where he was. There's no way to know what Patrick was thinking at the time, but he didn't do as Harry asked and went in the water. He'd only just started to swim towards his Mum when he got caught in a rip. Emma was facing the other way and didn't see him, or even know he'd come into the ocean.'

'Didn't Harry go in after them when he came back and realised?'

Catherine shook her head. 'Harry can't swim.'

As she drove home that night, Sophie thought about what Catherine had said. Tim's death had been an accident and Emma's, more than likely, hadn't been. That didn't make the grief any less. Or the guilt. When it came to guilt, she, probably more than anyone else, understood how Harry would have felt. Before Tim left on that fateful day, she was about to tell him to stay and to go tomorrow. But she hadn't because she knew he was keen to go. And so, he had. And not come back. So many times, she tormented herself with the thought that she should have opened her mouth and convinced him to stay home that afternoon.

Pulling into the driveway, she saw headlights coming towards her. She'd forgotten that Ryan said he'd be working late, as he'd been out of town for the past few days and wanted to make up lost time. Even though it still felt like a strange thing to do, she was glad she'd remembered to leave the door unlocked. It was something she'd have to get used to. Like a lot of other things.

As the car approached, it slowed down, then came to a stop. Ryan rolled down the window and waved.

'I've fixed the loose skirting boards in the third bedroom.'

'Thank you. I really appreciate all the repairs you're doing.'

'That's ok. Repairs like that are easy. Even some of the bigger jobs around here aren't that hard. It's a great house and it will be good to see everything back to how it should be.'

'Did you know the Andersons?'

Ryan nodded. 'I saw them whenever I came back to town. One of the brothers is the same age as me. We spent time together on my holidays. They'd all gone by the time I moved back though.'

'Even after being away for many years, you must know everyone in town.'

Ryan nodded. 'I do. And it wasn't my choice to grow up somewhere else. But it was my choice to come back.'

Sophie nodded. 'It's important to make the choices we feel we need.'

Ryan kept his eyes on her. 'Yes, it is. And sometimes those choices have you thinking about doing something you thought you'd never do again.'

And with that, Ryan rolled up the window and drove off, leaving Sophie wondering what he'd meant by those words. There were too many conversations with Ryan lately that left her wondering and while on one hand, it was maddening, on the other, she was intrigued.

Sophie was still speculating the following morning when she pulled into a parking spot near the store. She had time to spare before she needed to go in, so she decided to stroll along the main street. Even though she'd been in town for a while now, she'd only ventured into the stores she'd needed to and hadn't walked from one end to the other.

Starting on the left-hand side of the wide bitumen road, much wider than any road she'd seen in the city, a road with angled parking at the kerbs and parallel parking in the middle, she wandered along, waving to people she knew. Sophie passed a café, a bakery, a hardware store and a post office, which also doubled as the local bank branch. Crossing the road, she saw Maggie standing in the doorway of the grocery store and Sophie waved. She still had a couple of minutes, so she stopped to say hello.

'Lovely morning,' Maggie said, a grin spread across her face. 'Spring has officially started.'

Sophie beamed too. 'I love spring. It's my favourite season.'

Then she turned and looked at the road behind her. 'I noticed the trees in the middle and along the edges of the footpaths are starting to flower.'

Maggie nodded. 'Won't be long before the street is a burst of colour. It would be nice if they stayed like that all year, but as we know, seasons come and go.'

Sophie considered Maggie's words for a moment. They were true of both nature and people, and she was trusting that one day, her change of season would arrive. She didn't say that to Maggie though.

'Ready for your day at the store?' Maggie said, bringing Sophie back to the moment.

Sophie nodded. 'I was a bit early, so I thought I'd go for a walk but it's almost opening time so I can't chat for long.'

'Yes, we're both at the mercy of opening and closing times. I wouldn't swap it for anything though. It may only be a general store in a small country town, but it's mine. I own it and I love it.'

For the second time in just over a minute, Sophie paused to consider Maggie's words. The library where she used to work had opening and closing times but there'd been a roster, so she'd taken it in turns with the other librarians. Here it was only herself and Catherine and lately, on occasion, Catherine had been coming in later than usual. It was then up to Sophie to open the store.

She'd been thinking recently about some small changes she'd make if the store was hers. But it wasn't, and being aware of how much Catherine was a fixture in this town, Sophie didn't feel like she'd around long enough to suggest changing anything.

'I'm looking forward to the next book club,' Maggie said as Sophie turned to go. 'I've almost finished the book.'

Sophie smiled as she walked off, glad that people were enjoying the book club. She was too and it was a nice feeling.

Unfortunately, her smile didn't last long as Harry was the first customer of the day. No matter how much she'd tried to be nice to him, he was still frosty whenever he saw her. But as she watched him open the door and walk towards the counter, what Catherine and Bev had uttered about Emma came to mind. So instead, she tried to focus on how she could befriend Harry. Not an easy thing to do, but after everything he'd been through, she felt like it was worth trying.

'How are you today, Harry?'

It wasn't words that Harry used to respond, but the grunt he emitted, along with the general demeanour that was enough to let Sophie know.

He stood and watched her make the coffee in silence. It wasn't until he turned to go that he spoke.

'I don't normally share my personal business with people, so I'd appreciate it if you keep anything I've told you to yourself.'

'Of course.'

She would have expressed more, but before she had the chance, he left.

Thoughts about her very short conversation with Harry were still in her mind when the door opened again. This time, it was Ryan. He wasn't a regular in the store, so she was surprised to see him.

'Morning Ryan. Is there something I forgot about the repairs?'

Ryan shook his head. 'I needed to come into town to get a few supplies and thought I'd get a coffee before I went home.'

As Sophie made the coffee, she realised it was the first time he'd come into the store and ordered a coffee. She'd made him coffee when he was at her house. But he'd never come into the store to buy one.

'I'll get one of those slices as well,' he said, pointing to the top shelf of the cabinet. 'Did you make them?'

Sophie shook her head. 'Not today. Bev made those. It's my turn tomorrow to provide the sweet treats.'

'I might have to come back tomorrow then,' he said with a grin. 'Something to look forward to.'

'I'm still perfecting my baking skills so don't look forward to it too much.'

'I'm sure you wouldn't be supplying the store tomorrow if you're baking wasn't up to scratch. And from everything I've tasted, it is. Anyway, there's more to look forward to than just baking,' he said as he walked out the door. 'See you tomorrow.'

'Something on your mind?' Catherine asked, as she entered the store not long after.

Sophie shook her head. She didn't want to share the thoughts that were racing through her head. And as much as she'd tried to keep them from showing on her face, she obviously hadn't been successful. Sophie could tell Catherine didn't believe her, but she didn't push the point.

After Catherine went through to the office in the back, Sophie stood still for a moment and stared out the window. It wasn't just thoughts about Ryan and the confusion she felt, that were swirling around in her mind. Since he'd left the store, memories of Tim had come cascading back, mostly recollections from the time they were first getting to know each other.

Those first few dates, so different to any she'd had previously. By the third date, she knew he was someone she could go the distance with. Instead of just booking a restaurant, he'd organised a picnic at sunset, preparing all the food himself, three courses of it, and bought a bottle of champagne to go with all the delicious cuisine. A blanket on the ground and candles at the ready for after the sun went down completed the picture. It wasn't just coming up with the idea for their third date, it was also the effort he'd put in that impressed her and made her realise he was someone who sincerely wanted to see where a relationship could go.

As they watched the sunset, Sophie had felt completely relaxed, both by the setting and by how comfortable she was with Tim. It was a beautiful memory. Now, as she let the images from that day float across her mind, there was extra sadness attached to them. Not only did they not go the distance she thought they would, but the site of the picnic had been a cliff top, overlooking a beach, the same beach he'd gone to the day he didn't come home. She hadn't been back there since.

Continuing to stare out the window, Sophie suddenly wished for the vibrancy of the city. In the country, where she now found herself, there wasn't enough going on to distract her from the memories. And from why she was thinking about how relationships started.

After closing the store that day, Sophie proceeded to Jess' house after a quick detour to pick up Molly.

'Do you feel like you've settled into life here?' Jess queried, as they departed on the walk they'd planned earlier in the day.

Sophie deliberated for a moment before responding, the words needed to answer Jess' question not coming with any sense of clarity. 'I'm getting there. I don't feel like this is completely my home yet, but I don't feel like it's not either. If that makes sense.'

She was surprised when Jess nodded. It didn't make sense to Sophie yet.

'This is a huge change for you. You can't expect everything to fall into place straight away.'

For the next few minutes, they strolled in silence and Sophie contemplated what Jess had said. And realised she was right. Ever since Sophie had arrived, she'd been trying to rush things, to push herself into making this town her home instead of letting things happen naturally, in their own time.

And then Jess spoke again. 'I hear Ryan has been into the store a few times.'

Sophie glanced over, only to observe a grin spread across her friend's face.

'What's are you grinning about?'

Jess shrugged nonchalantly. 'I don't know what you're talking about.'

Sophie laughed. 'Yes, you do.'

'It's obvious to me that he likes you.'

Sophie didn't say anything, instead picking up her pace, putting distance between herself and the words Jess had uttered.

'I might be wrong,' Jess said, catching up with Sophie. 'But I don't think I am, and I know you're probably not ready to hear that, but I thought you should know.'

Sophie kept walking, eyes straight ahead. Jess was right. She wasn't ready to hear that. When she finally stopped, she turned back to Jess.

'I don't think you're wrong, but it's too soon.'

Jess put her arm around Sophie's shoulders and looked directly at Sophie's face. 'Is it?'

That question entrenched itself in Sophie's mind for the rest of the walk. She could also tell that Jess was debating the wisdom of speaking, rather than remaining quiet. The only one on the walk without a care in the world was Molly. The puppy stopped to sniff every tree, running back and forth across the path, each time something grabbed her attention, or stirred her sense of smell. But no matter how distracted she was, Molly stayed close to them, turning around every now and then to make sure Sophie wasn't too far away.

As she watched Molly sniff her way along the path, Sophie thought how easy life was for a puppy. Food and water, shelter, exercise, love. Things people needed too, but those things were only the beginning of a much longer list, some of the entries bringing joy, others bringing only pain.

On the way back from Jess', Sophie decided she didn't feel like cooking that night. In recent weeks, she'd been expanding on the basic repertoire she'd been relying on to give her sustenance and thrown in a few meals here and there that required more ingredients and more effort to prepare. As a result, tasted better than the basics. So, she swung by the house to drop Molly off, much to her dislike, if the look of indignation on the puppy's face was anything to go by. Sophie hadn't realised, before she became

147

Molly's owner, that dogs could display such looks, but it hadn't taken her long to realise they could. Molly was very good at making Sophie feel guilty whenever she went out and left her puppy behind.

Just like her first night in town, she drove past the pub and pulled up in the RSL car park instead. And like that first night, Jim was there. He was sitting by himself, so Sophie went over and asked if he wanted company.

'Well, this is a treat,' he said as she sat down.

Sophie smiled. Since she'd come to Hillford, Jim had been nothing but kind, much like everyone she'd met, except Harry, who she still couldn't figure out. So, she asked Jim about him.

Jim laughed. 'You're not the only one who's asked me about Harry over the years.'

Sophie smiled. She could believe that.

'Don't pay him no mind. Under that exterior, he's a good person. Life has just been cruel to him a few times over the years, so he pretends to be hard-hearted. The reality is, he's one of the gentlest people I've ever known.'

'You must have known him a long time.'

'Since school. We both grew up in the same sort of home. Not much in the way of material possession, but plenty of love.'

Jim paused for a moment and Sophie could tell he was remembering those years. After a few moments, he chuckled, then continued. 'And a lot of hard work. Up at dawn, chores around the farm before school, then more chores when we both got home. His family's farm was next to mine. We both hated those chores when we were young. It's only after we became adults that we realised we were doing about a tenth of what our parents did.'

'I didn't realise Harry grew up on a farm. He's never mentioned it. I assumed he'd grown up in town.'

Jim shook his head. 'The stories I could tell you about us as youngsters, our lives dictated by whatever the needs of the farms where on any given day.'

'You still have yours,' Sophie stated. 'Why doesn't Harry have his?'

'Farming was never in Harry's blood. On the other hand, his younger brother wanted nothing more than to take over the farm.'

'I've never heard Harry mention his younger brother.'

'His brother was killed in an accident on the farm, many years ago now. After it happened, Harry didn't have the heart to try and talk himself into taking over. So, he sold the farm. It weighed on his mind for years, selling the family farm. But it was the right thing to do. He was never cut out to be a farmer.'

'What sort of accident was it?' Sophie enquired. 'If you don't mind me asking.'

Jim shook his head. 'It's public knowledge so Harry won't mind me telling you. His brother, Bill, was out in one of the fields when the tractor he was on shuddered to a halt. He jumped out to see what the problem was when it suddenly lurched forward and ran him over.'

'What a terrible tragedy,' Sophie uttered.

She was still thinking about it when their meals turned up. More grief in such a small town. It seemed to be becoming a theme. Although, she realised, there was just as much grief and tragedy where she came from, more so, given the population. But here, with everyone knowing everyone else, it had a personal element to it, stirring all those in the community. And Harry, grieving not once, but twice, and possibly other times she didn't know about. On top of that, he'd sold the farm, in a community where everyone knew it had belonged to his family for generations. It gave Sophie more insight into why Harry was the way he was.

'Time to change the topic,' Jim said, putting down his cutlery. 'You must be settled in now. What do you think of our little town?'

Sophie smiled as she responded. 'I can see why Hillford won the friendliest town award.'

Jim laughed. 'Well deserved I say. We may be small, but we are friendly. Even Harry.'

As they ate their meals, they continued to chat, and Sophie enjoyed every minute of it. Jim was good company, and she felt relaxed, almost as if she belonged here. Once the plates were cleared away, Sophie went to stand up, thinking it was time to go, even though part of her didn't want to.

'You're not leaving now, are you? Bingo is about to start.'

'Bingo,' Sophie said with a puzzled look on her face.

Jim smiled. 'Every Wednesday night. That's why I'm here. I enjoy it. I've been coming for years. Have you ever played?'

Sophie shook her head.

'You don't know what you're missing out on. Stay and I'll show you the ropes.'

Why not, she thought? She hadn't really wanted to go anyway.

'You'll be given a paper board with fifteen numbered squares. Roy, who is our caller each week, will randomly select one number at a time and then holler them out. If you've got the number he calls out, mark it on your card. Whoever marks off all the numbers on their card first calls out "bingo".'

Sophie smiled. She may not have played before, but she knew how the game worked, as she assumed, did most people. It was kind of Jim to explain though, so she didn't say anything.

'As well as being a bit of fun, bingo is supposed to be good for you as you get older. Keeps the mind active and it's a good way to socialise with others and be a bit competitive at the same time.'

It only took a few minutes after the game started for Sophie to realise how enthusiastic some of the town's people were when it came to bingo. There was good natured banter, lots of laughter and a lot of shouting. And some of the good-natured banter came her way. It built on her earlier feeling that she belonged here. On top of that, she was starting to believe that people were happy she'd chosen their town as the place to become the latest resident.

As the game progressed, the more passionate the participants became, and the more the laughter continued. The host helped the laughter along by using catchy phrases to announce each number like 'naughty forty' and 'legs eleven'. Even though everyone in the room would have heard those phrases many times before, they still cheered every time a number was called out.

To Sophie's surprise, her card was filling up quickly and she only had one number left. Roy continued to call out numbers, but none were the number she wanted. It appeared they weren't the numbers anyone else wanted either because no one called out bingo. Number after number came out, but still no one said the magic word. Until, finally, Roy called out the number Sophie needed. And she yelled "bingo".

'Good for you,' Jim declared, cheering her on. 'And for your first game to.'

Sophie smiled, thinking how much she'd enjoyed herself. 'Thank you.'

From the moment the game started to when it finished, she'd been laughing and having fun. For something she hadn't tried before, she'd had a wonderful time. And felt part of the community.

'You know you win a prize.'

Sophie shook her head.

'It's usually a meal voucher for here, or money to spend at the bar. Something that keeps the dollars in the venue. With the financial hardships some people are dealing with, not as many people come in for dinner as they used to. A night out is a luxury for some at the moment.'

Sophie pondered Jim's words as she drove home. She would have thought books were a luxury that wouldn't be on the top of the list if money was tight. But people still came into the bookstore. She decided to mention it to Catherine the next day and see what she thought.

'Yes, books are a luxury for a lot of people,' Catherine replied when Sophie asked her the question.

'So why do we have so many customers still?'

Catherine smiled. 'I mustn't have told you about the unofficial town library.'

Sophie shook her head. 'What's that?'

'A lot of our customers, once they've finished the book they've bought, they give it to one of their friends to read. And then that person gives it to the next person and so on. So, the one copy of a book goes through several hands.'

'That explains why people only buy one book at a time. They all share with each other.'

Catherine nodded. 'That way they can continue to read without spending too much money.'

'Maybe we could share the books we read for book club once the meeting is over.'

Catherine nodded again. 'I had the same idea, but I keep forgetting to mention it at our meetings.'

Sophie smiled. 'Between the two of us, I'm sure we'll remember.'

Even as she said it, she doubted Catherine would forget anything. So, the only conclusion Sophie could come to was that Catherine wanted it to be Sophie's idea. Another way to get her involved in the town perhaps.

As the day went on, Sophie took more notice of those that came in and the book they bought, and she wondered who would get the book next and how many people would get enjoyment from the same story.

She also wondered what other things like that happened in town. Sharing in that way or doing something nice for someone else. She didn't know then, but not too far into the future, she would be roped in to help with an activity that focused on doing something nice for more than just a few people. And she would end up being in charge.

Chapter Nine

'I heard you had fun at bingo last night,' Maggie said as Sophie walked into the supermarket later that day.

Sophie laughed. 'I should know by now that there isn't anything I can do in this town that everyone won't find out about.'

Maggie laughed too. 'I'm sure it's taken a lot for you to get used to. But it's not in a bad way. We just like to know that those we care about are ok.'

'There's no one in town that you don't care about, is there?'

Maggie shook her head. 'I know it's different where you come from. But we know each other, grew up together. There's nothing we wouldn't do to help someone out. The people here are our family.'

When she'd first arrived in town, that was a foreign concept for Sophie. But now she was beginning to understand it. And feel it.

'How are the repairs going?' Maggie asked as Sophie filled up her trolley.

'Really well. I think Ryan will be finished soon.'

'I figured he must be. He's been there a lot.'

Sophie was about to ask how she knew that, until she remembered.

'I'm lucky he was available to do the work.'

'Yes, Ryan is always in demand. And not just for work.'

A smile began to spread across Maggie's face before she changed her expression. But Sophie had seen it. And knew what Maggie had been thinking. The same thing Catherine had been thinking. And that Jess had articulated.

'I heard his last relationship ended badly. I assumed that's why he doesn't have a girlfriend.'

Maggie nodded. 'Yes, but it's probably time he stopped being alone.'

'I'm sure he won't be once he feels ready. Sometimes that takes a long time.'

Maggie squeezed Sophie's hand. 'I'm sorry. Have I upset you?'

Sophie shook her head. 'I just know what it's like when people want you to start dating again when you're not sure you're ready.'

Maggie nodded. 'I can understand that. But I think Ryan is ready. Enough time has passed. He's just waiting for the right person.'

Behind them, the door opened, distracting Maggie's attention. For which Sophie was grateful. On one hand, she felt like she was being pulled along a path she wasn't sure she was ready for. On the other, she was beginning to feel like it's where she should be heading.

'I'm looking forward to book club tonight,' Maggie said when she came back. 'I loved the book.'

Sophie nodded. 'Me too. It's one of my favourites, which is why I added it to the list. But you already knew that.'

Maggie smiled. 'Yes, but I can see why now. How many times have you read it?'

Sophie grinned. 'Several times. I found my copy when I was unpacking and thought it would be a good addition to the books that I'd already picked. I hope the others like it too. I would hate to suggest something that turned out to be a chore for people.'

Maggie shook her head. 'I'm sure no one thought reading it was a chore.'

Sophie was about to reply when more customers walked in. Instead, she just said she'd see Maggie that night at the bookstore and walked out with her groceries. And with thoughts of Ryan on her mind.

After the store closed for the day, Sophie stayed back to set up for book club. As she placed her copy of *The Blind Assassin* by Margaret Atwood on her chair, she smiled, thinking how much she was looking forward to that night's meeting.

Once everything was in place, she spent a few minutes wandering around the bookstore. In each section, she could see her touches. It was still very much Catherine's store, but her influence was there for people to see. And for her to begin feeling that this really was her job, and she was meant to be where she was.

Pam was the first to arrive, followed by Bev, then Jess. Maggie and Catherine came in together. For a fleeting moment, Sophie detected a look that passed between the two of them as they walked in the door, one that was gone as quickly as it came, before she could try and decipher what it might be about.

'Catherine helped me put together the food platters for tonight,' Maggie said as she and Catherine placed them on the table.

'Yum,' Jess pronounced, surveying the offerings in front of her. 'And you didn't have to go far to get all the ingredients.'

Maggie laughed. 'Grabbed everything from the shelves just before I closed the doors.'

Pam peered down at the platters. 'It may have been quick to get the ingredients, but it looks like you spent a lot of time pulling all this together. Everything looks delicious. I don't think there'll be anything left.'

'Thanks Pam,' Maggie said. 'I can't take all the credit though. Catherine was an amazing help.'

Catherine smiled. 'It was my pleasure.'

And then, again, Sophie caught a glance they shared, and she got the feeling there'd been a discussion of some sort, while they'd been putting the food together.

'Everyone ready to get started?' Sophie said, turning her mind back to the reason they were all there.

Around the room heads nodded.

'Who'd like to go first?'

'Why don't you go first, Sophie,' Maggie suggested. 'We know it's one of your favourite books.'

'If I go first, no one else will get a word in.'

Catherine turned towards her. 'That's ok. I'm sure everyone is happy to wait for their turn.'

'Ok, but don't say I didn't warn you. First off, I love the way it's written. I feel like I get lost in the language. And I love the 'novel within a novel' and the revelation that the protagonist is not who you first think it is. It's very clever.'

Maggie chimed in. 'I liked that too. The way this book is constructed is very different to any others I've read. I admire the author's talent to be able to pull that off.'

Bev agreed. 'It took me a while to get into the style but once I understood it and realised what was happening, I was hooked.'

Sophie breathed a sigh of relief. 'That's good to hear. I was worried I'd suggested a book that people didn't like. It might be one of my favourites but it's probably not for every reader.'

Catherine shook her head. 'You certainly didn't do that. I think it's safe to say from the number of notes we all have in front of us that we enjoyed it enough to come prepared with plenty to talk about.'

Pam nodded in agreement then continued the conversation.

'Even if we hadn't, I'm sure with all the books we're going to read there'll be ones that either some of us, or all of us, don't like. Look at the differing opinions on the last book.'

Sophie knew Pam was right. The idea of everyone liking every book was not realistic. And a book club should have differing opinions. There'd be no discussion otherwise.

'So, what were some of your thoughts?' Sophie asked, looking at the women seated around the table.

Jess was the first to jump in, her eyes travelling around the room, engaging with each of the other members at some point while she was talking. 'It was a melancholy read. The betrayals, the guilt, the suicides, the affairs, the references to war. All the things that happened to Iris and Laura as well as how awful some of the other characters were. All the characters were screwed up in one way of another.'

And then she swivelled to face Sophie. 'I still enjoyed it though.'

Sophie grinned. It was sweet of Jess to say. On reflection, it wasn't the usual style of book Jess enjoyed, but the way she said those last few words led Sophie to believe that she meant it. So, she continued on from what Jess had said.

'Yes the characters are all strange in some way, bordering on unbalanced in the case of a few of them. But something that stuck out from what you just said was the references to war. This is the third book we've read that had a war theme running through it, and like the first book we read, this one references the Second World War as well. The recurring theme was accidental though. I picked the books at random.'

Bev reached forward to grab a snack from the trays on the table. 'It doesn't bother me.'

'It hasn't bothered me either,' Pam said, following Bev's lead and reaching for the trays.

Catherine nodded. 'It's fine with me too. The Second World War references were something I was particularly interested in as I was reading, but that's because of my history, which I shared with you when we read *The Guernsey Literary and Potato Peel Pie Society.'*

'It wasn't anything deliberate on my part,' Sophie reiterated. 'But it is a reminder that for books set in certain time periods, the story is informed about what was going on in the world at the time. And in the 1940s, nothing had more influence, in a negative way, than the war.'

Bev nodded. 'It was interesting though to hear the mentions from a Canadian perspective. Like us, most of what our country and our people went through at that time is overshadowed by the British and the Americans. But even in this small town, we remember, and hold services on Anzac Day and Remembrance Day. The Remembrance Day services will be on again in a few months' time, in November.'

Sophie made a mental note to attend. It was important to show her respects. She was sure she'd already met most of those who had family members names engraved on the memorial which stood in the park at the end of the main street.

'Apart from war, which we've discussed in other meetings, what else stood out as themes?'

Maggie spoke first. 'Well, Jess has already mentioned betrayal and guilt, but they were two themes that stood out for me as well.'

Pam bobbed her head in agreement. 'And I'll also second Jess' comment about the characters. Some of them were horrible. But to me, that's a reflection of real life. There are people that you're happy to have in your life and then there are those you stay right away from. Especially those that hurt you, although hopefully, not as badly as some of the characters.'

And with those words, Sophie's mind turned to Ryan, even though she hadn't planned on that happening. How badly had he been hurt? To distract herself from those thoughts, and from wondering, again, why she was interested, she asked for other thoughts about the book.

'I found it interesting discovering the relationship between the girls and their housekeeper,' Bev said. 'If those girls had come from a poor family, there may have been no one to care for them after their mother died.'

Catherine concurred. 'They may have ended up in an orphanage, which were terrible places back then. Although, coming from a family with money didn't stop more awful things happening to them during their lives.'

Pam agreed. 'You can't buy happiness as the saying goes.'

'The other part I relished,' Jess added, 'was discovering that the protagonist wasn't who I thought it was, but her sister instead. It was very clever the way that was done.

Sophie smiled. 'I adored that too. It's a complex book, but the first time I read it, I enjoyed finding out all the details and how everything fits together. I enjoyed it this time too.'

Pam turned toward Sophie. 'Yes, it was complex, but I liked that I had to concentrate as I read. There have been some books I've read where I haven't needed to concentrate at all.'

Maggie nodded before adding to what Pam had said. 'I've read plenty of books like that too. But they have their place. Sometimes, especially when life is busy, all you want is to be entertained for a while.'

'True,' Pam said. 'And it's also true that just like this particular book, life can be complex too.'

Sophie knew all too well how complex life could be, especially when it gets turned upside down by an incident you weren't expecting. But in the past few months, since she'd arrived in Hillford, life had become simpler, if only because of the location. Yes, the people in town were dealing with all sorts of things, as Sophie was starting to discover. But the town itself didn't make life more complicated than it needed to be. There was a reason she found herself here when she could have gone anywhere. Maybe the simple life was what she needed, not just now but into the future.

'One more thing I wanted to mention before we finish tonight,' Sophie said, an hour later when everyone's notebooks had been put away and the discussion had concluded. 'Catherine and I talked about sharing the books we read at book club with others through the unofficial town library.'

Around the room, everyone nodded their heads.

'Great idea,' Bev said. 'I'll start distributing my books tomorrow.'

Maggie nodded. 'I'll do that too. I'll take mine into the store and make them available to anyone who comes in.'

'That's a great idea, Maggie,' Jess said. 'Pam, you and I could take ours to school and see if any of the parents would like to read them.'

'Yes, let's do that. I'll bring mine with me in the morning.'

As Sophie looked around the room, she was glad that the books they read would be shared with others and hopefully, bring them the same pleasure that it had brought those seated around the table. Well mostly pleasure. Some of the topics they'd discussed so far had produced mixed feelings in some of the participants. But at least they'd been books that triggered a lot of discussion.

At the end of the night, when Sophie and Catherine were cleaning up, Bev also stayed behind to help. Although, as Sophie was soon to discover, she had an ulterior motive. 'You've been in town a while now and there's something I've been meaning to get you involved in.'

Catherine chuckled. 'I'm surprised you waited this long.'

Bev pivoted to stare at her. 'Enough of that Catherine. You know this is serious.'

Sophie was apprehensive, until she saw a grin appear on Bev's face.

'As you know,' Bev began. 'I'm president of the local CWA and I think it would be good for you, and for us, if you joined.'

'I don't know very much about the CWA.'

For a moment, Sophie thought she'd said the wrong thing but then Catherine came to her rescue.

'Of course you don't. It's the Country Women's Association, not the City Women's Association and you've spent your whole life in the city up until now. Why don't you tell her all about it, Bev?'

As Bev began to speak, it was easy to hear the passion in her voice.

'The largest rural and regional advocacy group in Australia. That's how it's described. It's been around since 1922, starting in New South Wales, followed not long after by Queensland. Back in the time of the Great Depression, CWA members helped those in need by providing food and clothes. During the second World War, members did a lot to support the war effort by making and mending uniforms and camouflage nets that could be sent to the troops. They also provided catering when the troop trains came through on the way to the ports where the ships departed. On top of that, they bundled up care packages to send to those who were serving overseas.'

Sophie's mind was filled briefly with images of women, dressed in the clothes of the 1940s, sitting in a hall adding each item to a care package, before wrapping it tightly prior to its long journey by sea to the other side of the world. And as those images drifted through her mind, she also wondered how many of those women had husbands or sons that would receive a care package. Probably not one that had been packed by their wife or mother, but by someone else's. And she also wondered how many of the men who received a package came home again.

'Nowadays, as well as helping those in our community that need it, we award student scholarships and help some of our older members navigate the challenges of modern life', Bev continued. 'The national level CWA no longer exists unfortunately, but the state ones do. Women need to stick to together out here. Without us, the whole place would fall apart. Our chapter has been running for over one hundred years.'

When she finished speaking, Sophie smiled at Bev. 'That's sounds like something I definitely want to be part of.'

'Glad to hear it,' Bev said. 'Oh, and before I head off, Jess is going away for a week over the September school holidays, so I'll need someone to start filling in on the baking roster for the bookstore. Catherine said you'd been practising your baking.'

Sophie watched as Bev headed out the door, aware that Catherine was trying not to laugh behind her.

'You should know by now how persuasive Bev can be,' Catherine said. 'I've yet to meet anyone who can say no to her.'

Sophie nodded, a grin spreading across her face. 'She didn't even give me a chance to say no. I'm glad I've been doing some trial runs.'

Catherine smiled back at her. 'I'm sure whatever you bring in will sell out in no time.'

After Sophie got back to the house, she pulled out the box of cookbooks again. This time she didn't cry as she went through them. Towards the bottom of the box, she found one that had recipes for baked sweet treats that she hadn't tried yet and put that book on the counter.

She also kept a couple of cookbooks out that contained the recipes for her favourite meals. As she flicked through them, she decided her first test run would be with Jess. It was about time Sophie returned the favour and prepared dinner for her. And when she'd finished, she put those recipe books on the shelf near the stove and threw the empty box in the bin.

Chapter Ten

The sound of a car on the driveway let Sophie know that Ryan had arrived. So far, she was extremely pleased with how the repairs were going at her house. Then, as she opened the door, she paused for a moment, realising that it was the first time she'd thought of it as her house without immediately dismissing the thought. And she realised that she felt ok with that.

'Afternoon,' Ryan said as hopped out of his ute and grabbed his toolbox from back.

'Thanks for coming today,' Sophie said.

'Not a problem. I had to come into town this afternoon anyway.'

Sophie tried not to chuckle. He didn't live that far out of town and even if he didn't have any errands to do, he still could have easily got to her place in under fifteen minutes. If they were back in the city, where she used to live, fifteen minutes meant she'd still be stuck in traffic no more than the next suburb away, with her calculating whether she'd be late in reaching her destination. As she watched Ryan walk through the front door, she wondered if her destination was closer than she thought.

While he worked, Sophie busied herself in the kitchen, having settled on a new recipe she found in one of her cookbooks. If she finished baking in time, she would ask Ryan to be her taste tester again, although considering how many treats she'd backed lately, she probably didn't need to do anymore practice runs. But for some reason, she continued doing them, especially on the days Ryan came over to work on the house.

'All done for today,' Ryan said, strolling into the kitchen an hour later.

'Thanks, I really appreciate the work you're doing.'

Ryan shrugged, as if to indicate that the repairs were nothing out of the ordinary for him. 'Something smells good.'

Sophie pointed to the tray she'd just taken out of the oven. 'A new sweet treat I'm attempting, before possibly taking it to the store. If it turns out as good as what the recipe promises it will, that is. Did you want to try some?'

Ryan grinned. 'I was hoping you'd say that. I've loved everything you've baked so far. You've got the knack for it.'

Sophie would be lying if she didn't admit to herself that his praise gave her a warm glow. To Ryan, she just said thank you and then cut a wedge from the chocolate coconut slice.

'Just give it a minute though,' she advised as she handed it over. 'It's very hot.'

But he ignored her recommendation and bit straight in. A few seconds later, he dropped the remainder on the bench and then drained a glass of cold water.

Sophie couldn't help herself and chuckled at his reaction. 'I told you.'

'I know, but it smelt so good. I couldn't help myself.'

'I'll wrap some up and you can take it home.'

'Thanks. You know I'll enjoy every bite.'

'That's nice of you to say.'

'And if you ever need a guinea pig to taste test any other new recipes, I'm your man,' he said with a grin. 'Or if you've got leftovers, happy to help with those as well.'

Sophie laughed. 'I'll keep that in mind. I'm sure an opportunity will come up.'

'How about this Sunday? I was thinking of going out to the dam for a swim. Did you want to come along? We could have a picnic lunch while we're there.'

'Won't it be too cold to swim? Spring only just started a few weeks ago.'

Ryan shook his head. 'I don't know why, but the water in the dam is always warm.'

Sophie nodded. 'Ok, that sounds like fun. I haven't been out there yet.'

'Great. I'll see you on Sunday. 11am? Then we can swim before we eat.'

Sophie nodded. 'Sounds like a plan. I'll bring food for lunch.'

Ryan grinned. 'I was hoping you'd say that. Also, I don't want to subject you to my cooking skills.'

Sophie smiled too. 'I knew there was an ulterior motive. And I'm sure you're being too modest about your cooking. You feed yourself every day, don't you?'

Ryan nodded. 'Yes, but just basics. I can't do anything complicated.'

'Nothing wrong with the basics, and the more complicated dishes, that's just practice.'

'I'll have to get some pointers from you some day.'

Sophie smiled again. 'I'm sure I can manage that.'

Ryan hesitated for a moment and Sophie had the feeling he was going to say something else, but he didn't, instead gathering his things before heading out the door. As she watched him get in his ute and head down the driveway, it dawned on her that what she was doing on Sunday could possibly be considered a date. Had that been Ryan's intention when he suggested it?

The thought of a date scared her more than she was willing to entertain. It was far too soon. Instead of dwelling on the thought, she decided to ask Jess when she came over for dinner that night. In the meantime, she changed her focus to the meal she would be preparing prior to Jess' arrival.

'Am I reading too much into it,' Sophie checked, only a few minutes after Jess had come through the front door. She hadn't even sat down yet.

Jess shook her head. 'I don't think so. I've never heard of him going to the dam with any of his friends. It's somewhere he likes to go by himself, to have time on his own. He's always done that. It's somewhere special to him.'

As Sophie let Jess' words sink in, she thought back over her interactions with Ryan. Had she said or done anything that indicated she wanted to be more than friends? And if the dam was a special place to him, one he frequented on his own, what other reason would he have for sharing it with her?

'Oh no,' Sophie sighed. 'What have I done?'

'Nothing you shouldn't be doing. Go along and have fun. Maybe we're both wrong. Now, here's a wine I picked up on the way. I think we both could use a splash.'

As Sophie reached for the wine goblets, she wished she could go back in time, just a few hours, and say no to the picnic. Since agreeing to go, all she'd felt was confusion, when what she really needed was clarity.

'Something smells delicious. What's for dinner?'

Grateful to Jess for changing the subject, she filled their glasses and then answered.

'Moroccan stuffed eggplant. It's a dish I used to cook regularly but I haven't prepared it for a while. It was one of Tim's favourites.'

Jess put her arm around Sophie's shoulder and gave her a squeeze. 'Thank you for cooking it for me. I appreciate it and I can't wait to taste it.'

Over dinner, Sophie raised the topic of Ryan again, even though that hadn't been her plan. 'I heard his last relationship ended badly.'

Jess nodded. 'He was really happy and then she broke his heart.'

'And he hasn't had a relationship since?'

Jess shook her head. 'Why? I thought you weren't interested in anything like that?'

Sophie sighed. 'I'm not. Or maybe I am. I don't know. One minute I feel like I'll never be interested in anyone again, then the next I think maybe I will. I'm just second guessing why he asked me to go on the weekend.'

'I guess you'll find out when you get there,' Jess teased.

'Aargh! Don't say that,' Sophie groaned. 'That makes me more nervous than I already am.'

'There's nothing to feel nervous about. Just go along and have a good time. You'll know what to do if you start to feel uncomfortable.'

For the rest of the meal, they chatted about many other topics but didn't revisit the conversation about Ryan.

'So do I get the full tour now?' Jess said with a grin after they'd finished the main course.

Tonight was the third time Jess had come to the house, but the other times had been quick drop ins over a cup of coffee, and the most Jess had seen was the kitchen, hallway and verandah. Now that the meal was underway, she could add dining room to the list.

'And the stuffed eggplant was so delicious that I've eaten too much and now feel uncomfortable. I need a break before you bring out what I'm assuming is a cheese platter based on what I saw when you opened the fridge to put the wine back.'

Sophie laughed. 'I know how much you like cheese, so yes, I put a platter together. But we can do the tour first.'

As they wandered through the house, Sophie started to feel a sense of pride in her new life. The house was beginning to feel more like home as each day passed, and her possessions, instead of appearing out of place, looked as if they belonged.

'How are the repairs going?'

And with those words, Jess brought the conversation back to Ryan.

'I'm pleased with the work that's been done. It's coming along nicely.'

'So, Ryan's been here a few times now, hasn't he?'

Sophie nodded. 'Yes, and now that's enough of that topic of conversation. I'll go and get that cheese platter. We can sit on the front verandah.'

'Just because we're leaving the topic of conversation behind, doesn't mean that I don't realise you'll still think about it. If you need to talk at another time, I'll be here.'

While Jess headed outside, Molly trailing behind, Sophie realised what a good friend she had. Not wanting to leave Jess outside too long on her own, she put the finishing touches on the platter and headed out of the kitchen.

As Sophie stepped out onto the verandah, she noticed that Molly was snuggled contentedly on Jess' lap.

'You know she won't willingly move from there.'

Jess gazed down at Molly, while patting her at the same time. 'I know, but she's adorable.'

'Don't I know it. That's how she gets away with so much.'

They stayed outside until the cheese platter and the last of the wine had gone. Even though she'd been in town a while now, sometimes Sophie was still taken aback by how quiet it was. And how beautiful it was to stare up at the stars, observing how brightly they shone away from high rises and streetlights. As Saturday turned into Sunday and then Monday arrived, Sophie tried to hold on to that peaceful feeling, but as each weekday came and went and the weekend got closer, it dwindled at a faster and faster pace.

By the time the day of the picnic rolled around, Sophie had wound herself up into such a state that she almost cancelled. But then she pulled herself up and in a stern voice, one that was confined to her head, proclaimed that it was time to stop being silly. She was not a thirteen-year-old and it was just lunch and a swim. She was overthinking it; she was sure of it. Working herself into a state for nothing.

With that firmly planted in her mind, she picked up the basket with the food she'd prepared, climbed into her car and headed off in the direction of the dam. It was only when she was almost there that she'd heard a noise, a soft whimper. Then out of the corner of her eye, she saw a nose, a very familiar nose. Somehow, as she'd been loading the picnic basket and towel into the car, Molly had snuck in. She must have been hiding on the floor behind the driver's seat. If she turned around to take Molly back, she'd be late. Instead, she sighed and continued driving. It would have to be three for lunch.

As she got out of her car and took in the landscape around her, Sophie regretted not coming here sooner. The dark blue water that rippled across the surface of the dam; the tall, native trees which provided plenty of shade across the vast expanse of flat ground; the soft, green grass underfoot; the whole area surrounded by rolling hills. Those elements combined to deliver a picturesque spot for a picnic, a stroll, or a hike, depending on the mood of the day. Or it could just as much be a place to come and let her thoughts drift away.

As she stood there, taking deep breaths, she was glad she came early to have a few minutes to herself before Ryan arrived. When his car pulled up, she told herself there was nothing to worry about. It was just lunch and a swim. She'd said those words before, but she needed to keep repeating them. When he hopped out of his car, Molly's ears pricked up and she sprang over towards him. When she reached him, it was clear that Ryan was happy to see the energetic puppy.

'I didn't know you were bringing Molly,' he said, crouching down on the ground and scratching the dog behind her ears.

Sophie figured the only thing she could do was come clean. 'I didn't know I was either. She snuck into the car while I wasn't looking, and I didn't realise until I was almost here. For such an energetic puppy, she managed to remain remarkably quiet for most of the journey.'

Ryan laughed. 'That's not surprising. It's something her dad used to do when he was younger. One day, I drove into town to go to Maggie's store, and I didn't realise until I parked outside and opened the car door to get out. Then his head popped up and he just looked at me, as if he was wondering why the car had stopped. He loves being in the car, especially with the window down so he can stick his head out.'

Sophie smiled. 'I feel better now knowing I'm not the only one this has happened to.'

'I bet you didn't think you'd be swimming when you moved here,' Ryan said as they reached the spot at the edge of the dam where they were leaving their towels. Molly had already gone in and was paddling near the shore.

Sophie shook her head. 'I'm looking forward to it though. I used to swim at the beach regularly and I miss it.'

'Well, there aren't any waves, and it's not salt water, but I think you'll enjoy it. I come here all the time, and so do a lot of the locals.'

Sophie looked around her. She could see several other people there, including Bev, who she knew would already have spotted Sophie's companion for the day. And who would be very curious the next time she came into the bookstore, preparing her questions before she walked through the door.

'Do you still want to swim first?' Ryan checked, interrupting her thoughts.

Sophie nodded. 'Yes, let's swim and then eat.'

Ryan smiled. 'I can't wait to try the food you've brought. If it's anything like the treats I've had so far, it's going to be delicious.'

Sophie thought about the food she'd prepared–a smoked salmon frittata, chicken and asparagus scrolls, a fresh garden salad and a small cheese platter to finish–and how much she'd enjoyed making everything. It had been a long time since she'd taken the time to potter around the kitchen, slowing down and taking pleasure in everything she prepared, rather than rushing to get a meal done.

'How long have you been coming here?' Sophie asked as she pulled her towel out of her bag.

'Ever since I was a child. Even if I had no one to come with, every time we came back for the holidays, I'd gravitate here. This place has a lot of good memories and it's important to me.'

'That's great that you have a place like this. Thank you for sharing it with me.'

Ryan smiled. 'That's ok. It's not exactly a secret spot, but still, it's been a long time since I invited someone to come here.'

'Well, now you've shared it with two of us,' Sophie said pointing to Molly, not sure what else to say.

And with that, she walked down to the water's edge, not wanting the conversation to continue on its current tangent. As she dipped her toes in, she immediately comprehended what Ryan had said about the water temperature. It was perfect. Not too cold, but with a slight chill so it didn't feel like she was about to hop into a warm bath. She'd never liked swimming when the water was warm. Tim had been the opposite. He'd hated swimming when it was too cold. To him, warm water was comforting, making him feel like he was a child again. But to Sophie, if the water had a slight chill to it, she felt like her body was alive. Had that been a portent for what was to come?

Floating away from the shore, Sophie pushed those thoughts aside and instead, stared up at the clear, blue sky and white fluffy clouds. Ryan was using the time as he wanted as well, languidly swimming from one side of the dam to the other, chatting with her each time he went past. Sophie could have done the same, but she was content to paddle around the one area, using the least amount of energy as possible. She also couldn't be bothered going out deeper where she couldn't touch the bottom when she needed a break from paddling.

Sophie could easily have stayed there for hours, letting the water hold her up, surround her and comfort her. The only thing that finally got her out of the water was her grumbling tummy. That and the fact that Molly kept swimming towards her wanting to play and interrupting her peace. And she could no longer ignore the stares she and Ryan were getting from others, both in the water and from the shore.

As Ryan laid the picnic blanket he'd bought with him on the ground, Sophie pulled the containers of food out of the basket, along with the plates and cutlery.

'Wow,' Ryan declared. 'This looks amazing. Good thing I bought a bottle of wine to have with lunch.'

Sophie observed him as he poured two glasses, feeling the nerves begin to reappear. It doesn't mean anything she told herself. It's just a drink to go with the meal.

The first few sips were taken in silence, with Sophie pretending she was looking at the view around her. As well as the wine, she was still thinking about what Ryan had said about not inviting anyone else to this spot before.

'It's a great spot, isn't it?' Ryan said, disturbing the stillness, and Sophie's thoughts.

Sophie nodded. Obviously, she was being convincing with her pretend focus.

'Are you hungry?' she asked, turning to look at him across the blanket.

Ryan enthusiastically nodded. 'Let's eat.'

All through lunch, Ryan made positive comments about the food. Even though she was a little uneasy, it still felt nice to be complimented. It had been a while since she'd heard any compliments from a man.

'I had heard before today that you didn't always live here,' Sophie said. 'When did you move back?'

'Seven years ago. I should have made the move a long time before that.'

'Is that because you missed being here?'

Ryan nodded. 'This is my home, even though I was away for many years.'

'What was the reason your family moved in the first place?'

'Dad walked out on us when I was six, so mum became the sole provider for me and my brother. Jobs in the city paid more than they did here so that's where we went. I wanted to stay but I was a child, so I didn't have any say in matter. I had to go where mum went.'

'I'm sorry to hear that your dad walked out.'

Ryan shrugged again. 'It was a long time ago.'

'Do you have a relationship with him now?'

Ryan shook his head. 'I haven't heard from him since the day he left.'

Sophie was shocked when she heard that. She knew people who'd been divorced but she'd never met anyone whose parent had walked out, never to be seen or heard from again.

'I hope I haven't upset you asking that. I didn't realise. I wouldn't have asked if I'd known.'

'It's fine. I came to terms with it a long time ago. And everyone else in town knows so there's no reason you shouldn't. I'd rather you heard from me anyway. As much as l like everyone here, a lot of people tend to exaggerate stories.'

Sophie smiled. 'I have noticed that.'

Even as she said, she was reminded of how glad she was that not many people knew her story. That she knew of that is. In a town like this, more people probably knew about Tim than she was aware of.

'Still, I'll never move again. The only reason I didn't come back earlier was there was someone I thought was special in the city. But that turned out not to be the case.'

'I'm sorry to hear that too.'

Sophie remembered what she'd heard from Catherine and Bev and even though she didn't have the whole picture, she had enough to know not to ask any further questions.

'What about you?' Ryan said. 'Moving here is a big change for you.'

Sophie was trying to decide how to answer when they were interrupted.

'What are you doing here?'

Sophie didn't need to turn around to recognise the voice.

'Nice to see you too Harry,' she replied in her sweetest voice. 'How's your day going?'

Harry grunted but didn't say anything in response. Instead, he turned to Ryan and asked if he could bring his car in the following day. There was a noise, and Harry didn't know where it was coming from. After settling on a time, Harry turned and walked away. But not before admonishing Molly who was just trying to be friendly and obtain a pat or two.

Sophie watched him as he left before turning back to Ryan. 'For some reason, he doesn't like me.'

Ryan shook his head. 'It's not you. Harry doesn't like anybody. But once he gets to know you better, he'll tolerate you like he does everyone else. He's had a sad life.'

Sophie nodded. 'He told me about his family.'

'Everyone who knows him says he hasn't been the same since. It must be an awful thing to go through.'

That was Sophie's cue to dish up the last course and change the topic. As far as she knew, Ryan didn't know about Tim and now wasn't the time to mention anything. She'd started to relax as the meal progressed, and she didn't know whether it was the surroundings or possibly the company. Whatever it was, Sophie didn't want to think too much about it. She just wanted to enjoy it. But then everything changed in an instant. Ryan leaned over and kissed her. And Sophie froze.

'I'm sorry,' Ryan said, flustered. 'I shouldn't have done that. I thought... Are you ok?'

Sophie, still in shock, nodded slowly. 'I don't think I'm ready for anything like that. It's too soon.'

'Too soon from what?'

Even though she hadn't planned on saying anything about Tim, she had to talk about him. It wouldn't be fair to Ryan otherwise. So, in as few words as possible, Sophie described what had happened.

'I didn't know. I'm sorry that happened to you.'

'So am I.'

As soon as she said it, she realised how true it was and wished more than anything that she could go back and change the past.

'I think I'll head home now,' Sophie muttered, while hurriedly packing up the picnic basket.

As she walked away, Molly close at her heals, she knew Ryan was watching her. She didn't turn around though. Any vague thoughts she'd had recently about maybe being ready to see someone new flew from her head the minute he kissed her. She'd been fooling herself. She wasn't ready.

On the drive back, Sophie turned down the road where the town's cemetery was located. She'd never taken this route when returning from previous outings further afield, even though it was the quickest way back into town. It may have been a long way from where Tim was buried, but she knew the sight of the headstones would bring the image of his grave into sharp focus. But that day, she took a deep breath and indicated, needing to get back to the house as quickly as possible so she could shut the world out.

As soon as she turned, she spotted Harry's car, parked under a tree near the entrance. She debated whether to stop, but then she saw a solitary figure, standing in amongst the gravestones and she slowed down, then pulled over. Harry was standing there, his shoulders drooping. And she couldn't leave him there on his own. If he wanted her to leave, she would. But something was telling her to go over to him, even in amongst the grief that was seeping into her being.

Harry turned his head only briefly in acknowledgement when Sophie came up beside him. He didn't say anything and neither did she. Instead, Sophie read the names and dates on the headstones—Emma Smithfield, 1950-1992; Patrick Smithfield, 1980-1992.

'Do you visit Tim's grave?' Harry asked, still looking down at the resting place of his wife and son. 'Or his memorial?'

'His grave. I used to go regularly when I lived in the city. I haven't been since I moved to town. How often do you come here?'

'Only a few times a year now. After it happened, I came all the time. But over the years, that's changed.'

Harry was quiet again for a few minutes, before speaking. 'I still miss them. I remember that day like it was yesterday. I remember Emma walking into the water. And I remember her telling Patrick to stay with me. That she wanted a few moments by herself. She repeated it more than once. She didn't want either of us going in with her. But Patrick did.'

Then he turned and walked back to his car.

After watching him go, Sophie turned her attention back to the two graves in front of her and she wondered how Harry and Emma had met and how long they'd been married. And if Harry had been a different, happier person before his wife and child died. And in amongst those thoughts, memories of Tim's funeral came flooding back.

As Sophie had looked around that morning, she remembered how sunny it was and how that seemed wrong. It had been too bright, too jolting. And she remembered looking at the crowd, shocked initially by how many had turned up. But Tim had many friends and acquaintances, always taking time for the people in his life. He would stop and chat with everyone. And on that sunny morning, everyone he'd ever chatted with seemed to be there. And they all wanted to talk to Sophie, to console her. Which was a waste of time because nothing could console her.

She'd sat in the front row and without ever turning around, she knew all eyes were upon her. She could feel it. Time went slowly, slower than Sophie ever thought it could. She managed to hold the tears in until the photos rolled across the large screen at the front of the room. The photos of Tim as a child were manageable. Even some in adulthood were ok. But when the first photo of the two of them together appeared, tears began to roll down her cheeks, streaking her face. Those behind her had been unaware as Sophie made no sound. She didn't have the energy to. The only sign was her wet cheeks. And her eyes which continued to well over.

Sophie composed herself for a few minutes but started to cry again when the music started. Songs she'd been asked to choose. Songs that meant something to Tim. One of which was by a band he'd been a fan of and that he'd asked her to go and see with him on one of their early dates. As she sat there, an image took hold of her mind. The two of them in a small, crowded venue, lights shining on the stage, the house lights dimmed, waiting for the band to take the stage. Tim had his arm around her. It had felt nice but not familiar yet. They'd listened to the music, and all the while, Tim had a smile on his face. A smile he'd later said was because of her as well as the music.

When the service was over, all those in attendance came up to her, one after the other. Thinking back now, she couldn't remember the words those people had shared with her, or what she'd said in return. But she did remember how every one of those people hugged her. And how much she'd hated it, a reminder that Tim would never hug her again.

Afterwards, when the location had changed to the graveyard, the memory of the conversation she'd had with Tim about his wishes was front and centre in her mind. He'd said that he wanted to be buried rather than cremated. It was a family tradition he'd said, and he wanted to continue it on. Sophie hadn't taken much notice, thinking it was a morbid discussion to be having, and also, one that didn't need to be had for a very long time to come. Turned out, that wasn't the case and even in amongst her grief, she was at least glad that she knew what Tim's wishes were so she could follow them, no matter how much she wished she didn't have to.

As she'd left the graveyard, it had occurred to her that it was the first burial she'd ever been too. All the other funerals she'd attended had been cremations.

She'd drifted through the wake, never feeling like she was actually there. It was as if she was floating, watching from above. She observed people standing in groups, eating, drinking, talking. As she watched the conversations around the room, she could tell who the people were that had thoughts running through their heads like *'what if it had been me?'*, *'I'm older'*, *'I go to that beach all the time'*. Others acted like they'd done what they'd came to do and now that the funeral service was over and they'd put in appearance at the wake, they could get on with their lives. Is that what Sophie was expected to do? Get on with her life. How was she supposed to do that?

When it was all over, Sophie went home and slept. And stayed in bed the following day as well.

For the next three weeks, she continued in a daze. It was the fourth week when she started to feel something other than grief. When she realised she had to pick herself up and continue on, it was disconcerting.

By the fifth week, she got dressed and went into the library. Everyone there told her to take as much time as she needed and that she should go home if she wasn't ready to be there. Being there was what she needed though. She needed to keep her mind occupied. She didn't want to spend entire days crying anymore. And she didn't want to stay in the house by herself. That's how she'd started to think of it. A house. It wasn't a home anymore.

It had taken several more weeks of moving through life in actions but without thought or connection before she'd first begun to think about where to from here. And the first time the idea of starting again in a different location popped into her mind. But it was several months after that she finally made the decision.

That night, her mind racing with thoughts that she couldn't make sense of, she turned her attention to the sweet treats recipes she had decided on for her first foray into supplying the store—a raspberry and coconut slice and salted caramel brownies. Making those would keep her occupied for a while.

When they were done, she didn't know what she'd do to take her mind off the afternoon's events or the memories that had followed.

Chapter Eleven

'Morning,' Bev called out, as she opened the door of the bookstore. 'I saw you at the dam yesterday. Did you have a nice time?'

Sophie could tell by the tone of Bev's voice that what she really wanted to know was did she have a nice time with Ryan. But how could she answer that? So instead, she just replied that it was a lovely spot and that she should have gone sooner. Then she turned her attention to the trays she was putting in the cabinet. Behind her, she could tell Bev was debating whether or not to say something else. Eventually, she reached for the small pieces of slice that had broken off and were left on the tray, filling her mouth instead of using it to interrogate Sophie.

'You have to make all the treats from now on,' Bev exclaimed, as she sampled the raspberry and coconut slice, after already tasting the brownie. 'These are both delicious.'

'Must be beginner's luck,' Sophie said.

Bev shook her head. 'Rubbish. You've got a talent for this. And we've got one of our cooking committees next week so I'm putting your name down.'

Sophie hesitated, used to cooking for only a couple of people at most, not the larger number that Bev had previously mentioned the committee cooked for.

Catherine, seeing the look on her face, moved to reassure her. 'You'll be fine. We won't be cooking anything fancy for the number of people who'll be there. It will just be easy dishes.'

Sophie turned to look at her. 'The number of people who'll be where?'

'I'd thought I'd mentioned that,' Bev said, knowing full well that she hadn't, waiting instead for backup from Catherine. 'We're holding a fundraising dinner in the town hall for some of our farmers who've been doing it tough as a result of the drought.'

'A fundraising dinner?' Sophie queried. 'But won't people expect something nice if they're coming to donate money?'

Catherine nodded. 'Nice yes, but you know most of the people here now. They have no time for the sort of dishes they serve in fancy restaurants in the city where a large plate comes out with only a small amount of food placed in the middle with greenery served on top. And then charge you a fortune for.'

Bev nodded. 'We'd have a riot if we served something like that. What we need is something that people are unlikely to cook themselves at home, but not too different to the food their used to eating. I'm sure you'll come up with something, Sophie.'

'Me?' Sophie exclaimed, turning from one to the other.

'Absolutely,' Catherine said. 'It's about time we had something different to the usual type of menu we serve at these things. I think people are ready for something different.'

Bev nodded. 'But not to different, keep in mind.'

'I'm sure whatever Sophie comes up with will be delicious. And a big hit,' Catherine said.

Bev agreed. 'Of course. I have no doubt. Right, I'm heading off. I'll leave the menu to you, Sophie.'

Sophie watched as Bev walked out the door. What on earth was she going to do?

Catherine, having seen the look on Sophie's face, put her arm around Sophie's shoulders. 'You'll be fine. Don't panic.'

Easy for you to say, Sophie thought to herself as Catherine walked away. Then she sighed, realising that her night would be consumed with going through her cookbooks trying to find something a bit different but not too different. Whatever that meant.

As she stood in her kitchen, several hours later, was she still trying to figure out what it meant. After going through several cookbooks, she was beginning to despair. Then she came across a dish that might work for an entrée—chicken wrapped in prosciutto, with asparagus and cheese in the middle. She knew from meals she'd had at the RSL since she'd moved into town that dishes with chicken and asparagus were sometimes on the special's menu. Surely adding some prosciutto would count as a little bit different, but not too different. Sophie made a note on the piece of paper she was using to write down the menu. When it was done, she'd show Catherine and Bev and see what they thought.

An hour later, she was pleased that she had a complete menu planned. The chicken and prosciutto would be followed by a slow cooked beef ragu and then a tiramisu for dessert. The prosciutto gave her the idea for an Italian theme and after that, it had been easy. At least until she shared her thoughts with Catherine and Bev tomorrow. But she was feeling confident. Anything with beef would be a hit. And pasta was always a hearty meal, and hearty meals were popular in Hillford.

Even though she'd eaten at the RSL a few times since her arrival in town, she was still surprised each time she looked down at the meal she'd ordered, stumped by how the chef managed to fit so much food on one plate. And how the wait staff managed to bring it to her table without any food falling over the edge. Sophie used to feel guilty about wasting some of the food. There was just too much for her to eat in one sitting. But ever since Molly had come into her life, she'd been taking home the leftover meat from her meal in an appropriately named doggy bag, something her darling puppy was very appreciative of. Half the time, she wasn't even able to get fully out of her car before Molly started climbing up her legs, reaching for the food in her hands. Sophie knew it was a habit she needed to get Molly out of, but she looked so cute doing it that Sophie kept putting it off. Looking cute and the fact that Molly was so happy to see her and the love that was plastered across her little puppy face was something the Sophie needed every now and then.

As she read through the instructions for the ragu, memories came flooding back from the last time she'd cooked it. She and Tim. They'd laughed and talked and sipped wine. It was such a happy memory that she hadn't wanted to replace it. But now, it was time to cook the meal again. And add a new memory to the one that already existed.

Sophie arrived at the hall early and began setting up. Soon, the others arrived, all with their slow cookers in hand as requested. Sophie's menu had met with approval from both Catherine and Bev and apparently, the other women in the cooking committee who were all looking forward to bringing the menu Sophie planned to fruition.

'Right,' Bev said, clapping her hands to get everyone's attention. 'We've all got a part to play to get this ready on time. Over to you Sophie to get us going.'

Sophie looked around the room at the women of the CWA who had volunteered their time and cooking skills. Everyone was enthusiastic and itching to get started.

But just as Sophie was about to go through the instructions, she was interrupted by two unexpected arrivals, Harry and Jim.

'I know the cooking committee has only been women up to this point,' Harry said. 'But I think it's time the men got a look in.'

Jim nodded. 'We might pretend we can't cook, but we can. So, we're here to help.'

Sophie smiled. 'Everyone is welcome. The more cooks in the kitchen, the quicker we'll have the food ready for our guests.'

Bev nodded then pointed to a spare space on the bench. 'We'll get you set up over there and we'll soon have you put to work.'

Sophie waited until Harry and Jim were set up and then began the instructions. As she did, she walked around the room, stopping briefly at each person's cooking station. The slow cookers needed to go on first as it would take a couple of hours for the flavours to simmer together. Once that was under control, she went through the instructions for dessert. Harry and Jim could take charge of the chicken dish she decided. That didn't need to be cooked for a while yet, but it could be prepared and placed in the fridge ready for the frypans later.

The more time she spent in the kitchen at the back of the local hall, the more Sophie enjoyed herself. Everyone was content with her running the show, and comfortingly, they were all acting as if she'd always been there, rather than only appearing in their lives a few months prior. Even Harry. And as the afternoon progressed, she noticed a smile occasionally appear on Harry's face. Jim on the other hand, had been smiling since he'd arrived.

That feeling that Sophie had always been there continued as the afternoon turned to evening and the townspeople, dressed up for a change, took their places at the tables dotted through the main area of the hall. And it was hard to wipe the smile off her face.

'Wow,' Jess said as she and Sophie scanned the hall. 'All I'm seeing are empty plates. First course completed. The entrée was a big hit.'

As they continued to survey the tables, Harry and Jim came up beside them.

'Of course it was a big hit,' Harry declared. 'Jim and I did a great job.'

'I'll second that,' Jim said, grinning. 'Although we didn't do it alone Harry.'

'I know, but we were in charge,' Harry grumbled.

Sophie smiled. 'Yes, you were, and you did a fantastic job.'

Then she and Jess shared a glance between them, and when they turned back, Harry's demeanour had changed, and he seemed very pleased with himself.

Sophie then turned her attention back to the charity dinner attendees, sitting at their tables chatting away, having a wonderful time, waiting patiently for what would come next. 'I hope they enjoy the main course and dessert just as much.'

Jess squeezed Sophie's hand. 'Based on what we've just seen, I think it's safe to say they will. I told you there was nothing to worry about.'

Sophie let out a long slow breath. 'Thank you. I needed that.'

Even though Sophie had plenty of help getting the meal ready, ultimately, she was the one responsible for making sure everything was as it should be. She'd spent hours wandering around the kitchen, checking everything and tasting everything, helping with the cooking where needed.

'If I'd have known how a good a cook you were when I invited you over for dinner that first time, I would have prepared something much fancier.'

Sophie shook her head, thinking back to the lamb and rosemary pie that Jess had made. 'That dinner was delicious. You're an amazing cook.'

Before Jess could respond, Catherine appeared. 'I've heard nothing but countless compliments. Well done, Sophie. And look how thrilled Bev is.'

Sophie turned in Bev's direction and watched her for a few minutes. She was running around the room, gasbagging, checking people had everything they needed, all the while, her face lit up with joy.

'I'm glad she's pleased with how the dinner's going,' Sophie said. 'I hope we raise the amount she's hoping we do.'

Catherine nodded. 'I'm sure we will. Even though there are many here who don't have a lot, they'll still give what they can. They always do.'

Sophie thought about that for a moment. It was often the case that those who had little always gave something while those that had a lot, often gave nothing at all.

After the entrée plates had been taken away, there was gap of fifteen minutes before the main course was brought out. It gave those in the room a chance to wander over to other tables and talk with their friends and neighbours. But as soon the beef ragu came from the kitchen, everyone hurriedly took their places and turned their attention to the plates in front of them. As with the entrée, it didn't take long for main to disappear and along with it, all the worry that Sophie had felt leading up to the event.

When everyone had finished, Bev got up to speak while the finishing touches were being put on the dessert.

'Thank you all for coming tonight. I won't speak for too long, although you know that I can.'

Across the room laughter rang out.

'And I don't need to tell you the importance of why we're here, but I do want to thank you for everything you've contributed so far. We've raised more than I, or any of the others on the committee, were expecting and we're extremely grateful. Be assured that every dollar you've given will be put to good use, helping those who need it.'

A round of applause rang out.

'Before I finish, I also wanted to give a shout out to Sophie for planning the menu, cooking, galvanising our team of chefs and pitching in any way she could. Thank you, Sophie.'

The clapping started again, and Sophie couldn't keep the smile off her face. The feeling that she was part of something, that she'd been embraced by those in front of her, people she'd only met earlier that year, was heart-warming. These people had lived a life so different from the one she'd known. But now, their lives and hers were more similar than she ever would have imagined.

'One more thing before I sit down, as I'm sure you're all looking forward to dessert' Bev said.

Around the room Sophie could see a lot of heads nodding.

'I want to say a big thank you to our team of chefs, those ladies, and gentlemen, who volunteered their time this afternoon, making sure there was enough of the delicious food for everyone. Thank you, ladies and gents.'

Another round of applause rang out around the room. And Sophie felt happy, a type of happy she hadn't felt in a long time.

As she turned to head back into the kitchen to supervise the serving of dessert, she saw Harry and Jim talking to each other quietly. She had no idea what they were saying, but they both gave the impression that they were just as delighted as Sophie was. Although, given his usual demeanour, it wouldn't take a lot for Harry to look joyous.

By the time the night was over, Sophie had managed to speak, at one time or another, to each person in the hall. And with each conversation, no matter how brief, she felt the appreciation, and she gladly accepted the compliments.

One of those who complimented the meal was Ryan. She hadn't spoken to him since the night he'd rung, a few days after the picnic, to apologise again. But halfway through the conversation, she'd stopped him, saying it was kind of him to keep apologising, but once had been enough and he didn't need to keep doing it.

There had been other thoughts going through her mind during that conversation, thoughts she didn't share with Ryan. Like how, in the few days preceding the call, she'd been thinking that maybe, if things went very slowly, she might be ready. Maybe.

'What a fantastic night,' Bev proclaimed, the following morning as the last of the committee members walked through Sophie's front door. 'Everyone is still talking about the dishes that were served, Sophie.'

Sophie smiled, both from Bev's comment and the joy that lingered from the night before.

'You planned everything, directed us in what needed to be done and when, and kept the dinner on schedule. I'll have to put you in charge of the food next time as well.'

Next time, Sophie thought, had a nice ring to it.

'Right,' Bev said, interrupting Sophie's thoughts. 'Everyone's here so let's get started.'

As the CWA committee took their places around Sophie's dining room table, she made coffee and tea and brought out a plate of home-made biscuits.

'These are delicious,' Maggie declared. 'Did you get all the ingredients from my store or were there extras from somewhere else?'

'Where else would Sophie get ingredients from?' Bev snorted. 'You're the only grocery store in town. You supply everyone, including the CWA when we need it.'

Maggie turned to look directly at Bev, peering over the top of her glasses as she did. 'She might have ordered some ingredients online and had them delivered.'

Sophie grinned as she watched the two of them. It must be nice to have such a long-lasting friendship, one where they could both speak their mind, or rib each other when they felt like it. Catherine was the third part of the friendship triangle, but as Sophie had discovered since the day she'd first met her in person, Catherine could often be reserved, sitting back taking things in rather than taking part. Although, it had been Catherine who suggested the ladies meet at Sophie's place. Hesitant at first because it had only been Jess and Ryan who'd been in the house so far, she eventually agreed. More and more, she was beginning to think of it as her home, so it was time to invite others into it. And it would give her a chance to get to know the three other ladies on the committee, apart from Bev, Catherine and Pam, that she hadn't spent a lot of time with.

Bev reached over and grabbed a biscuit, dunking it in her tea then swallowing it, before beginning to speak. Although not without telling Sophie that she agreed with Maggie's assessment of the biscuits.

'Last night was the most successful fundraiser we've ever held. We raised $15,000.'

Around the room, a loud cheer went up. Seeing Sophie's confusion, Catherine leaned over and whispered that they usually raised only half that.

'So now we have a decision to make,' Bev said. 'We can support a few of the projects on the list we already have, or we can plan something new to fund.'

Sophie listened as the others discussed the possible options. Being new to the committee, she was happy to hear the discussion to get an idea of what the others thought might be the best use for the money they'd raised. The discussion went on for some time because there were so many great projects that could be funded, both existing and new ideas. But they had yet to reach a consensus on which ones to fund.

'All of the projects are worthy and it's too hard to choose between them,' Bev said, before turning to Sophie. 'You're new to this. Maybe a fresh perspective is what we need. Do any of the new ideas, or the existing projects you've heard about stand out? Or are there any new ideas you can think of that we haven't discussed?'

Sophie, aware that everyone was looking at her, took a moment before responding. 'There is one idea that isn't on the list but might be good for the town.'

And then Sophie spoke about a conversation she'd had with Jim not that long ago. He told her about the show they used to have once a year that brought people from all over the district together. As well as rides for the children, they had competitions for cakes, quilting, animals, art, and vegetables. He'd told her that it had always been well attended and that people looked forward to it.

Bev nodded. 'I remember the shows. They were a lot of fun, and yes, everyone looked forward to it and never planned anything else on the day the show was on. Jim's wife was on the organising committee before she passed away, so he would know all the details of how it was organised and run each year.'

'Why did they stop?' Sophie asked.

'They used to be sponsored by some of the big farming companies. Then the sponsorship stopped, and we couldn't afford it.'

Maggie scanned the room. 'We can now, if we contribute some of our time and resources as well as the money we raised. What do you think?'

Around the room heads nodded eagerly.

'I think it would lift people's spirits,' Catherine said. 'And bring people together, especially those that are on their own.'

Pam agreed. 'And bring back a sense of community too. With all the worries people have had over the past few years, trying to keep their properties running, doing something that will bring joy to Hillford is a great idea.'

'If we go ahead with it, do you think people will wonder why we didn't put the money to something drought related?' Bev queried, looking at the others.

Catherine shook her head. 'Even though we raised more than we normally do, it still isn't enough to do anything of significance that would help people on their farms. But giving people something to look forward to, I think that would be a good use of the money.'

Sophie had listened as the conversation went back and forth, glad she had suggested the show. She'd been doubtful before speaking but was now pleased that she had.

'If you're worried about what people will think about using the money this way, why don't we ask around and gauge what people think of the idea,' she suggested.

Bev nodded. 'Good idea. Sophie, you and Catherine can mention it to those who come into the bookstore, Maggie, you can mention it to people when they come and get their groceries. The rest of us can mention it to people we see on the street or in any businesses we go into. We can ask our neighbours too when we see them.'

With everyone in agreement, it looked like Sophie's idea might get off the ground, depending on the outcome of the soon to be had conversations around the topic that would take place outside of Sophie's house.

'Right,' Bev said. 'Now that's settled, we wouldn't mind having a look around. If that's all right with you, Sophie.'

Sophie, startled for a moment by the thought of the committee members poking around her house, but then realising there was no reason they shouldn't. It was time to share her house with everyone who crossed the threshold.

'I used to come here years ago when there were still Andersons living here,' Bev continued. 'I haven't been since the remaining family moved away.'

'What was it like back then?' Sophie said, wondering if her initial thoughts about the place were correct.

'Always something going on here. People coming in and out, lots of laughter, always food on the table for anyone who was hungry, a bed if anyone needed one for the night. A real family home, a place where everyone was welcome.'

It was a lovely image to have, but it left Sophie wondering whether the house would ever be like that again, in the time she was its custodian.

When they'd finished having a look around, the ladies took their drinks outside to the verandah, something Molly was very happy about. She'd never had so many people around and she was loving the attention. Sophie arranged her chair near the three women she wanted to get to know better so they could chat.

'I like what you've done,' Bev declared as she sat down. 'It still feels like the house it always was but now it has some of your touches too. I'm glad you haven't altered too much or filled the house with modern looking furniture. That would change the house too much. It's good that you can still feel the history of the place.'

Sophie wasn't a fan of modern looking furniture, as Bev put it, which was good because Bev was right. It would have looked out of place and impacted the character of the house. It looked like it belonged exactly where, and how, it was. And more and more, Sophie was having the same thought about herself.

'Seen anymore of Ryan lately?' Bev enquired.

And with those words, Bev brought Sophie back to the one subject she'd been wrestling with in her mind. Rather than deal with the confusing thoughts that had plagued her recently, especially while she was surrounded by others, she pretended not to hear and continued with the conversation she'd been involved in.

Chapter Twelve

For the next week, whenever a customer came into the bookstore, either Sophie or Catherine mentioned the idea of the show. To Sophie's surprise, but not Catherine's, everyone they spoke to was in favour of it, for all the reasons Catherine had mentioned. The idea of something to bring people together and lift their spirits was exactly what was needed. Similar responses were received by everyone else on the committee and before they all knew it, the decision was made that the show would go ahead.

Catherine suggested asking Jim to be involved seeing as he was familiar with how it had been put together in the past. Sophie thought that was a good idea, but she also knew Catherine had suggested it not just because of Jim's knowledge, but because she knew he was lonely. Jim had been a farmer all his life but since his wife passed away the previous year, he didn't have the heart for it anymore and his sons took over the farm full time, meaning his days weren't filled like they used to be. Catherine had already mentioned book club to him as she knew he liked to read. He'd been hesitant because there weren't any men involved but Catherine had reassured him that he would be very welcome, and that maybe he could bring Harry along. He'd looked sceptical but from where Sophie had been standing behind the counter, she could see he was considering Catherine's suggestion. Now she hoped he'd carefully consider the suggestion about becoming involved in organising the show as well and decided to come onboard. It would be good for him and for them.

The more she talked about the show, the more excited Sophie became. She'd never participated in anything like it so she wanted to be involved in any way she could. The fundraising dinner had not only given her confidence to take part in other activities in town, but it had also given her a greater desire to help the people of Hillford, many of whom were now her friends.

Later that week, she pulled up in front of the pub, ready for trivia night. When she walked in, she looked across the room and saw Ryan already seated at a table, talking with Jim. Ryan hadn't been back to the house recently, but she'd seen him several times since their picnic at the dam and every time, they stopped and chatted. Surprisingly, it wasn't awkward, like she thought it would be. Yes, there was a hint of something underneath the light conversations they had, but nothing that would stop them continuing. And every time they parted after those conversations, thoughts of Ryan kept creeping into her head, even though she'd tried to stop them.

It was during one of those conversations on the street that Sophie noticed the sign outside the pub advertising trivia, and she mentioned she'd never tried it before. Turned out, Ryan loved trivia, and he asked if she'd like to go. As friends he made a point of emphasising. Those words were more successful than anything she'd tried in stopping the thoughts that had been swirling through her mind.

'Hello, you two,' Sophie said, reaching the table.

'Hey Sophie,' Ryan replied.

'Evening,' Jim said, hopping up from the bar stool. 'I'll be on my way now that you're here. I don't want to interrupt.'

Sophie smiled. 'You're not interrupting. Stay and chat for a while.'

Jim shook his head. 'I need to head off anyway. I promised Harry I'd stop by. Enjoy your dinner and the trivia.'

'Before you go, at least tell me if you've given any thought to the conversation you had with Catherine.'

Ryan looked from one to the other before Sophie explained about wanting Jim to get involved in organising the show.

'You should do that, Jim,' Ryan said. 'You'd be great at it.'

'I don't know,' Jim said, hesitatingly. 'Isn't that a job for a younger person?'

Ryan shook his head. 'I think it's a job for someone with experience, like you. Think about how much it would mean to people to get the show up and running again.'

Jim looked first at Ryan then at Sophie.

Sophie nodded. 'Ryan is right. Say you'll do it, Jim.'

He slowly looked from one to the other again before nodding. 'Ok, I'll do it.'

Sophie reached over and gave him a hug. 'I'm so happy. I can't wait to tell the others on the CWA committee.'

For a moment, Sophie thought she'd embarrassed him, but then he smiled. 'I think it will be good for me.'

Ryan nodded. 'I think so too. In fact, I'll help you. I'd like to get involved as well.'

Sophie grinned. 'That would be great. The more people involved, the quicker we'll be able to pull the show together.

'Thanks Ryan. I'd appreciate the help. Now, I better go, or I'll be late. Harry doesn't like it when people are late.'

Sophie chuckled to herself. With what she knew of Harry, she could believe that. As she watched Jim walk away, she noticed that he wasn't shuffling like he usually did, and instead, she detected a spring in his step. The shuffling, Catherine had told her, had only come about after his wife died. The grief not only seeping into his mind, but into his body as well. Sophie had often wondered how he coped with his grief. It was a common thought any time she came across someone who had suffered like she had. And thinking about it now, she wondered what Ryan's exact circumstances had been. It hadn't been a death, but it had been a loss. She wanted to ask but wasn't sure if she should. Then she remembered that he knew her circumstances, but she didn't know his. So, she asked, and for a moment, she didn't think he was going to answer, given the look on his face. But then he did.

'Not much to tell. I thought we were happy. I know I was. She was too, just with someone else.'

'I'm sorry to hear that.'

Ryan shrugged. 'Nothing I can do about it. She made her choice, and I had to learn to live with it. And eventually I did. Coming back here helped.'

'That helped more than staying where you grew up?'

Ryan nodded. 'Yes, because whenever I came here, it felt more like home than my actual home. And the people, they don't stand for nonsense, and I like that. They say what they mean and there's no secrets.'

From the tone of his voice, she thought it best not to push for any more information.

'I ordered you a glass of wine as well as some snacks to tide us over until dinner,' Ryan said, before she had a chance to come up with a new topic to discuss. 'How was the rest of your day?'

Sophie could see the wine sitting on the bar, waiting for one of the staff to bring it over. It was thoughtful of him to do that, as well as order snacks. It's something a date would do, but that's not what this was.

'Was the bookstore busy?' Ryan continued after taking a sip of his beer.

Sophie shook her head. 'It was one of our quieter days. Not a lot of people came in. It was good though as it gave us a chance to tidy the shelves, do a stocktake and order some more books.'

'I didn't realise you had to tidy the shelves. Do they get messy very often?'

Sophie smiled. 'Not so much messy, but people are always putting books back in the wrong place so when the next customer comes along, they can't find the book they're looking for.'

Ryan nodded. 'That makes sense.'

'How was your day?' Sophie asked.

'Quiet too. Only two cars to work on today. If I had of known the store was quiet, we could have had lunch together.'

Was that as friends, Sophie wondered. It's not what she replied with though.

'That's ok. It took a lot of time to get the shop in order so I wouldn't have been able to take a long break anyway.'

Thank goodness to, Sophie said to herself. Twice in one day. That would have confused her even more. She was still conflicted when it came to the two options that could be possible with Ryan, although maybe it didn't matter anyway. Maybe friends was the only option he wanted after the events at the dam.

'We should order dinner,' Ryan said, interrupting her thoughts. 'It's busy tonight, so it might be a while before we get our meals.'

Sophie nodded. She was hungry. She hadn't eaten much at lunch because she'd been nervous about tonight. As she perused the menu, Ryan asked her if it was that she'd hadn't been to a trivia night at this pub or if she hadn't been to one at all. She and Tim had talked about going one night but they'd never got around to it. Another thing she would never get to do with Tim. But even though those thoughts were running through her head, the pain that constricted her heart was less.

Sophie shook her head. 'I've never been to any trivia night, anywhere.'

'You're in for a treat then. I've been coming since the pub started holding these nights,' Ryan said as he put down his menu, his dinner choice made. 'I usually go with a mate of mine, but he's headed off on an overseas trip.'

'That's exciting for him. It's been so long since I've been overseas.'

Again, memories of Tim swirled around in her mind. But this time, she let them float away.

'Have you been overseas?'

Ryan shook his head. 'It's something I've thought of doing many times. I just never got around to organising it. Or had anyone I really wanted to travel with.'

Sophie couldn't be sure but something about the look on his face made her think that maybe he saw her as someone he could do that with. Again, the confusion. It was so frustrating. Thankfully, before she could think about it any further, the trivia host came out, welcomed everyone and explained the rules.

Before the game started, Sophie had been apprehensive, thinking that she wouldn't know the answers and would sit there with a blank look on her face. But it turned out that she was good at trivia, answering more questions that she thought she would, and more questions than Ryan answered. Except for sport. She left all those questions to him.

By the end of the night, she realised she'd enjoyed herself more than she had in a long time. She almost told Ryan that but stopped herself at the last minute. Even though she'd had a great time, there was a small, quiet voice in the back of her mind, so quiet that she almost missed it, telling her that he probably did just want to be friends. And so, she kept quiet.

She continued to keep quiet the next time she saw Ryan, and then the time after that. The first time was when they had lunch in the bookstore during one of Sophie's breaks. She was aware of the looks they were getting from everyone who came in. But she'd figured they'd get looks anywhere they went. There was nowhere in town that someone wouldn't see them. The second time, they'd sat on Sophie's verandah after Ryan had finally come back to do some more of the repairs. She'd had a glass of wine, and he'd had a beer. And in front of them, the sun was setting. The setting had a distinctly romantic feel about it, something Sophie tried not to think about. As he got up to leave, he hesitated, as if he was going to say something. But at the last minute, he seemed to change his mind. She guessed she wasn't the only one who wasn't sure how to proceed. As she watched him go, she was thankful that she was heavily involved in the organising the show. Otherwise, she'd have too much time on her hands to think about her confusion.

That Sunday night, she had dinner with Jess and brought up how she was feeling.

'I'm one of the first to say Ryan is a lovely guy, but if you're not ready, then you're not,' she said. 'You can't force anything. That will never work. And from what you've said, it's not clear what he wants either.'

Sophie nodded. 'I know, I'm so confused. I don't know whether I can't make my mind up because I'm not ready or because I might be overthinking things and it's all in my head. Maybe he does just want to be friends and the kiss was a mistake.'

'What?' Jess spluttered, reaching for her napkin and dabbing her lips. 'He kissed you?' When?'

'The day we went to the dam.'

'And you didn't tell me!'

'I didn't tell anyone.'

Although as she said it, who else would she have told except Jess. Maybe Catherine?

'I just couldn't bring myself to say anything at the time.'

'No wonder you're confused. It makes more sense now.'

Sophie sighed. 'Yes, but it doesn't make the answer any clearer.'

'Have you thought about talking to Ryan? You'd know for sure then.'

Sophie nodded. 'I have thought about it. But what if I don't like the answer, even though I don't know what answer I'm looking for.'

The following morning saw the first meeting of the Hillford Show organising committee convene. Jim had come prepared, bringing all the notes and files his wife had used when she was the show president. And from what everyone saw as they went through them, there wouldn't be much else they'd need to do except follow what was written down.

Apart from Jim, Ryan, Sophie, Catherine, Bev and Maggie, surprisingly, Harry was also there. A few of the other women from the CWA were also in attendance. Jim took charge early on and divvied out that tasks that needed to be done. He put Harry in charge of organising the farm animal competition and the best pet competition, something he looked unsure of at first but one look from Jim stopped him from saying anything.

'Bev, you're fantastic at organising others, and getting a discount when needed.'

The others laughed as Jim said that. If anyone could get them a discount or something for free, it was Bev.

'Can you ring around and see what carnival rides you can get to come on the day. A few rides for the younger kids and a couple for the older kids.'

Bev nodded. 'Leave it with me.'

'Catherine, can I get you to organise the cake and quilting competitions?'

Catherine nodded. 'Happy to do that.'

'Maggie, I'd like to put you in charge of entertainment. Can you rustle up a few acts from around the district, or maybe even further afield that people can watch during the day?'

'On it.'

'And Sophie, can I put you in charge of the food? We'll need a few options for people to eat. I'm sure the other ladies here from the CWA would be happy to contribute.'

Sophie said that was ok with her and around the room, the other ladies nodded.

'Apart from the overall coordination, which Ryan has already offered to help me with, that leaves getting the showgrounds ready, which I can get some of the farmers to help with; seeing if I can get fireworks for the conclusion of the show at night; and rustling up prizes for the competitions.'

'I can help with all of those as well,' Ryan said.

'Thanks Ryan,' Jim said. 'I appreciate that.'

'Happy to help. I'm really looking forward to getting this show up and running. Again, a great idea Sophie. I think the whole town will be happy you've suggested it.'

As Sophie looked around the room, trying not to blush at Ryan's words, she could how pleased everyone was. Again, she had that feeling that she was now part of this town. This show was already doing what Catherine had said it would in bringing people together.

Over the next week, Sophie talked with all those who would be contributing to the food and came up with a list of all the different options that would be available and what sort of equipment they'd need on site. The next step would be to write the list of all the supplies they'd need to get from Maggie's store, including the ones she'd need to order in for them. With the amount of people the show committee hoped would attend, they'd need a lot more food than Maggie usually had in stock. But with the show planned for the start of summer, they still had time to come up with the list.

Thinking about the show had kept her occupied. But still, every so often, the words Jess said to her at their last dinner together floated back into her mind. And finally, she came to the decision that if she wanted any clarity, she'd have to do as Jess suggested and talk to Ryan.

As much as she was dreading the conversation, Sophie decided to talk to Ryan straight away before she chickened out. She didn't want to be anywhere in public, so, on the Friday, after she closed the store, she drove to his house, where she sat outside in her car for ten minutes before working up the courage to get out and walk to the front door.

Chapter Thirteen

'I need to ask you something,' she blurted out. 'Do you want to be just friends or something more?'

Ryan looked at her for a moment before responding. 'What do you want?'

Sophie would have preferred an answer rather than a question, but given what she knew of Ryan, and the fact that she wanted clarity, she would have to be the one to speak first. So she took the plunge.

'I'd like to see what happens if we become more than friends.'

'I'd like that too.'

'Why have you never said anything?'

'Why haven't you?'

He had a point. They were both adults, both able to say what they were thinking. Both too nervous to say anything.

'You don't have to answer that,' Ryan said. 'I know why you didn't say anything. The same reason I didn't. Neither of us wants a broken heart again.'

Sophie nodded. 'That's true. But I can't let it stop me anymore. I feel like I've been in limbo for so long, the weight of the grief holding me in the same place. I want to try and move forward.'

'Me too. So I guess it means we're giving this try.'

Sophie nodded again.

'Do you want to come in?'

Sophie stayed for two hours. They just talked, got to know each a little better. Nothing else for that night. It didn't matter that Sophie felt ready to try. She still needed things to go slowly. Very slowly.

The next morning, Sophie awoke to a sound she hadn't heard since she'd arrived in town. Rain. She could hear the beat of the raindrops on the tin roof. She jumped out of bed and looked through the window. Grey skies and clouds sagging with rain. She went to the front door, collecting Molly on the way, and then headed outside. She was still in her pyjamas, but she didn't care. She stood in the yard, holding Molly and let the rain wash over them both. Molly eventually wriggled out of her arms and rain back to the cover of the verandah. Sophie stayed and continued to let the water wash over her.

'I couldn't believe the rain this morning,' Sophie said as she rushed into the store, an hour later. 'It was amazing to see.'

Catherine, who was sitting at one of the tables, a coffee in her hand, nodded. 'It used to rain a lot in spring but not for the past few years. I hope it's enough to help the farmers.'

Something as important as the rains finally coming should have caused a more enthusiastic response from Catherine, but as Sophie observed her more closely, she could tell something wasn't right. Catherine looked tired, both physically and mentally. It was something Sophie had noticed a few days earlier, but when she'd mentioned it, Catherine had replied that she was fine. But Sophie could tell she wasn't, so she asked again. Catherine's answer was not what Sophie was expecting.

'I think I'd like to retire.'

Sophie pulled out the chair next to Catherine and sat down. 'How long have you been thinking about that?'

'I've thought about it off and on over the past eighteen months. It's only been the past six weeks though, when it turned into a continual thought. I opened this store forty-one years ago, you know. I remember people saying I was crazy at the time, but the store is still here.'

'Why did you decide to open it?' Sophie asked, still stunned by what Catherine had revealed.

But she kept that to herself as she listened to Catherine telling her about growing up on a farm, one of six children, four who had the land in their blood, and two that didn't. Two whose parents didn't understand the desire for something different, something away from the demands, all day, every day of the year, without a break, even though those same parents only became farmers after they arrived from London, the desire to be away from a city after what they'd endured during the war leading them down that path. But for Catherine, the stress of being at the hands of nature, drought one year, floods the next, worrying about food and water for animals, machinery that always needed tending to, never being able to go away for any length of time, all filled her with dread.

'Right up until the day they died, my parents never understood why I opened this store, why this was the right choice for me. Luckily, I had four brothers who wanted to stay on the land. They bought the adjoining parcels when they became available and expanded, working the business together. My sister left town. She wanted to see the bright lights. And she did. Made a success of herself in business.'

'Why now?' Sophie asked.

'Forty-one years is a long time. Not only have I managed this store, but I was a wife for most of those years, and a mother for many of them as well. I know people talk about work life balance now, but back when I was your age, women did it all. We worked and we looked after our families and our homes. After all these years, I'm tired. I've never had a long period of time off. Only the occasional holiday and they were never far afield. I'd like to try some new things. Take up a hobby. And I'm not as young as I used to be. It's getting harder to keep up with the hours.'

Sophie was silent for a moment, not sure how to take the news. Catherine had been there for her ever since she'd moved to Hillford. She'd seen her five days a week. And what if the new owner didn't need a store manager? What would she do?

'I can see I've shocked you,' Catherine said, reaching over to squeeze Sophie's hand. 'But there's one more thing.'

'I guess it's good that I'm still sitting down then.'

'I think you should buy the bookstore.'

'Me?'

'Of course, you. You manage the store so well; you know how everything works, and you know everyone in town now.'

Catherine was right about all those things, but buying the store was something needing considerable thought. And could she even afford it? More importantly, did she want to buy the store? She loved working there, but there was a big difference between just working and being the owner. Being an employee meant she could leave anytime. She couldn't do that as an owner. Although now things were progressing with Ryan, slowly as was her wish, that was something else that was tying her to Hillford.

'I know I've just given you a lot to contemplate,' Catherine said. 'Take some time to think about it.'

Sophie nodded, a myriad of considerations running through her mind.

'Does anyone else know?'

Catherine nodded. 'Only Maggie. We had a conversation a little while ago, before the book club where we discussed *The Blind Assassin*.'

Sophie remembered that night and how she'd thought they'd discussed something while preparing the food. If she had to guess what they'd discussed, retiring and selling the store would not have even come up as a possibility.

Later that day, Sophie sat on the verandah, Molly curled up quietly at her feet. That in itself was amazing. Still only a puppy, she'd got past the stage where she ran around like a whirlwind until she exhausted herself and then flopped down in a heap waiting for her energy to come back. Now she just ran around constantly, the only time she was still was when she was asleep. It was like she knew Sophie had something important to focus on. Everything around her was still as well, except for a light breeze. From her vantage point, she could see vast expanses of land and in the distance, the sun was starting to set, changing the colour of the sky to orange and pink.

She'd become used to life here and she liked it. She was a different person to the one who'd arrived in Hillford all those months ago. Thoughts of Tim were frequently with her, but she no longer cried. Maybe buying the bookstore and making Hillford her permanent home was the right thing to do.

It was too big of a decision for just one night though, so she picked Molly up and headed inside. She hadn't finished the book for the next book club and now was the perfect time to get stuck into a book and push the other thoughts out of her mind. She only needed the distraction for an hour as she was going to dinner with Ryan. He was taking her to a restaurant in a neighbouring town, which meant a long drive was involved. Sometimes, Sophie still forgot about the distances out here. You couldn't just catch an Uber to a restaurant in the next suburb like she'd done in the city.

But Ryan was keen to try this restaurant and so she agreed. She was still nervous sometimes about where the two of them were heading, but she owed it to herself to find out. So, after finishing a couple of chapters of the book, she opened her wardrobe and looked for something to wear. In the back were the dresses she used to wear when she and Tim went out. She stared at them for a long time before pulling one out. They were all so beautiful and they should be worn again. Picking one of them now was a good start. And she had a feeling that Tim wouldn't mind that she was wearing one. Or that she was going on a date.

Driving along the highway, in a direction that Sophie had yet to travel, she was surprised how much she could see by just the light of the moon and stars. Hectare after hectare of farmland, all empty as the cattle had gone into the sheds for the night. Letterboxes standing to attention by the side of the road, heralding the entry to the properties that lay behind them, most of them, a long way behind. Ryan was playing country music on the radio, something that Sophie had yet to get used to. As much as she'd tried, it wasn't her sort of music. But she didn't say anything, having already decided to suggest a different type of music for the drive back. On the way, their conversation centred around the show and all the planning and activities that were underway.

As they pulled into town, Sophie was surprised when Ryan told her it was twice as big as Hillford. She'd just assumed, wrongly as it turned out, that all the towns in this part of Western Queensland were about the same size.

Driving down the main street, Sophie could see a variety of shops and cafes, while parked cars took up most of the available parking spots. Ever since she'd moved, she'd never thought of what towns might be to the north or, like this one, to the south. She'd just presumed that she'd have to go back to the city to stock up on the things she couldn't get in Hillford, but maybe she wouldn't have to. Getting out of the car, she decided she'd come back in the daytime and have a proper look around. And maybe check the map and see what other towns in the region she could explore.

When they reached the restaurant, the door was opened from the inside and she and Ryan walked through. Looking around the room, she could see that every table was occupied. There was candlelight and white tablecloths, soft music in the background and wait staff gliding between the tables, unobtrusive but attentive when needed. It had been a long time since Sophie had been to a restaurant like this.

'Are you all right?' Ryan said, noticing the look on Sophie's face, which she'd unsuccessfully tried to hide.

Sophie nodded. 'I was just reminded of something. I'll be fine.'

'Tim?'

Sophie nodded again. 'I haven't been anywhere like this since he passed away. It just brought back memories.'

'Do you want to go?'

Sophie shook her head. 'I'll never forget Tim, but I can't keep living in the past. I need to look to the future.'

'Is that a future with me in it?'

At that moment, the waiter came to seat them. As they walked to the table, Sophie thought about what Ryan had asked. And sitting across from him, the answer was clear.

'Yes, I want you in my future. And my present. I still need to take things slowly though.'

Ryan nodded. 'So do I. I know what I went through is nothing like you did, but I still wish it hadn't happened.'

'I guess that's life though,' Sophie said. 'Things happen that we'd rather not happen. But after everything I've been through, I now realise there was nothing I could do to change it. So I have to find a way to live with it and make the most of what I've got.'

Two hours later, they were the last in the restaurant. Neither of them noticed until one of the waiters came over. As they walked out, Sophie thought how easy the past few hours had been. And it felt good.

Chapter Fourteen

Spring had well and truly arrived and the flowers in the gardens were blooming. Sophie had planted several different varieties and the colours that were now exploding across the garden beds created a stunning landscape. But not only that. They were the signs of new beginnings.

She'd woken up early and had been thinking about her date with Ryan since she'd got out of bed. She'd had a lovely time but after she got home, doubts started to creep in. At the restaurant she'd been sure she was ready to for a relationship but now she wasn't so sure. When she'd been with Ryan, she'd felt happy, a happiness that she hadn't felt in a long time. But now that she was away from him, guilt started to make its way in. Was she being disrespectful to Tim's memory? To Tim himself?

Still as she headed into store, she was content, figuring that things would work out as they were meant to. But the contentment didn't last long as she greeted the first customer of the day, Harry. Even though he'd been pleasant enough the past few times they'd seen each other, more so since the charity dinner, it wasn't a guarantee that the same would happen today.

'Would you like a coffee?'

Harry stared at her as if she'd said something stupid. 'Why else would I be here?'

Sophie refrained from responding, even though he'd come in before and bought food, and occasionally a book, without getting a coffee.

As she made it, she could feel him watching her, as if he was waiting for the right moment to say something.

After she handed him the coffee, he continued to stand on the other side of the counter, making no move to leave. So she prompted him.

'Is there anything else I can do for you, Harry?'

'What are you doing on Sunday?' he asked, the words tumbling out.

'Nothing planned yet. Why?'

Harry looked at her for a moment before responding. 'I'm taking some flowers to the cemetery. Will you come with me?'

For a moment, Sophie didn't respond, shocked that Harry would ask her along to something so personal. Then she realised, it was because she understood how he was feeling. And that he didn't want to go alone.

'Of course, I'll come with you. I feel honoured that you asked me.'

'Don't get carried away.'

Sophie fought to keep any sort of expression off her face. The gruff tone he'd just used was the Harry she'd come to know. But with this request, maybe she'd get to know a different side of him.

'I'll meet you there at 10 am.'

And then he was gone, before Sophie had a chance to say 10 am was fine.

For the rest of the day, the conversation with Harry stayed in the back of her mind. Catherine wasn't at the store that day, so Sophie didn't have to decide whether to mention her plans with Harry. But she did have to decide whether to take flowers with her.

Although, on reflection, she had a sneaking suspicion that Catherine already knew what Harry had been planning to ask her. Sophie wasn't the only to notice that Catherine and Harry had been spending time together lately. Sophie didn't know what that was about and she hadn't wanted to ask Catherine. Even though they talked about a lot of things, something told her not to ask Catherine about Harry.

By the time Sunday morning rolled around, she decided taking flowers was the right thing to do, so she called in to see Maggie on the way.

'This one is lovely,' Maggie said, holding up a bunch featuring pink and orange flowers. 'Emma loved these colours.'

'Wow. How did you know that?'

Maggie smiled. 'Small town, remember? And Harry used to come in and buy Emma flowers every so often.'

'I'm still a little shocked that Harry asked me to go with him today.'

Maggie nodded. 'It's out of character for him. But he's still struggling with grief all these years later. He's always kept it to himself. Maybe he's finally realised that sharing it with someone will help. And even though he won't admit it, I think he's lonely. It's been a long time. He needs someone in his life. But I'm sure I don't have to tell you that.'

Sophie nodded, but didn't say anything, not about Tim or her grief. Or about her suspicions about Catherine and Harry spending time together, although if something was going on, Maggie probably already knew. Instead, she asked Maggie how long she'd known Harry.

'For as long as I can remember. Like ninety percent of the population, I've lived here all my life. I don't recall what age I was when I first met him, but I would have been a child. I remember him coming into the store sometimes.'

'What were you doing in the store as a child?' Sophie asked, intrigued as to why a child would be interested in the comings and goings of a grocery store.

Maggie smiled. 'My parents opened this store not long after they married. Both their parents owned businesses in town, and they followed the tradition. Mum used to bring me in after school and I'd stay in the corner and play with my toys or do homework. When my parents no longer wanted the responsibility of running the store, I took it over.'

'Is that what you wanted to do?' Sophie asked, knowing that Maggie was an only child so there was no one else to take over.

Maggie nodded. 'I like being here, chatting to people every day, helping them get what they need.'

'Did your husband ever work in the store with you?'

Maggie shook her head. 'He had his own business fixing farm machinery. It's funny now when I think about it. I never wanted to be a farmer's wife, and he never wanted to be a farmer, yet he spent his working life on farms all over the district and I spent mine making sure those farmers had the supplies they needed to keep their families fed.'

Sophie smiled. 'So you are part of that life, but only on the periphery.'

Maggie smiled too. 'That's it. Obviously, I still am. But since my husband had the accident, he hasn't been to a farm.'

'How long ago was the accident, if you don't mind me asking?'

'Two years now. At first, he struggled with his new reality, but eventually he became himself again.'

Not for the first time since she'd come to town, Sophie reflected that there wasn't anyone who didn't have something going on in their lives, something that had changed the path they thought they were on, instead sending them in a different direction.

'He doesn't want to come in here and help out?'

Maggie smiled again. 'He's mentioned it a couple of times, but I've always said no. We work well together as a couple, but I don't think that would translate to business. Besides, what needs to be done to run this store, it's not him. Never was and never will be. It's just not his personality. That's why he always loved working on machinery. People want conversation, machinery doesn't.'

Sophie could understand that. As much as she and Tim had worked well as a couple, there was no way they could have been in business together. Their personalities were too different, and they would have driven each other crazy.

'Here you go,' Maggie said, handing over a bag containing the flowers. 'Good luck.'

As Sophie drove towards the cemetery, she thought about what Maggie had said about Harry keeping his grief to himself. She'd never really shared her grief with anyone either. She'd let bits and pieces show but nothing more than that. Maybe it was time she did that too. All hiding her grief had done was push it further down inside herself. After Tim had died and those first few weeks where she felt like she was barely existing, the only way she could carry on was to try and ignore the pain. Instead of dealing with the grief as it came, she forced it down. All that did was increase the time it took before she started to feel like herself again.

When she arrived, Harry was already there. He wasn't by their headstones but waiting under a tree.

'You're late.'

Sophie looked at her watch and saw that in fact she was early. She didn't say anything, but she was aware that Harry noticed her looking at her watch.

'We can walk over now.'

She was surprised that he'd waited until she got there before walking to their graves. But she realised Maggie had been right. He didn't want to be alone with his grief anymore.

When they reached the spot where Emma and Patrick were buried, Sophie placed the flowers down. The pink and orange bouquet first then the other one she'd bought for Patrick. She and Maggie had chosen white, orange and yellow for that. Even though Harry didn't say anything, the look on his face told her he was touched that she'd made the effort.

'I still feel guilty,' Harry said, breaking the silence.

'Why do you feel that way?'

'I should have known.'

It was the closest to an admission she would ever hear that Emma's death wasn't an accident.

'You still miss them a great deal, don't you?' Sophie asked, although she already knew the answer.

'Every day.'

'Did it ever get easier?'

'Eventually. But it never goes away completely. And I'm sorry again for the way I spoke to you that day in the store, when I said you shouldn't have come to town. I didn't mean it. Even since they passed away, I've been in a bad mood.'

From then on, they stood in silence. Harry didn't want to talk. He just wanted company. They stood for twenty minutes before Harry turned to leave. Sophie followed him back to their cars, then back into town.

On the drive home, Sophie's mind was filled with thoughts of Tim. Mostly happy ones, which made her smile. Others though, like when she'd had to organise the funeral, were not. And in amongst those thoughts, her relationship with Ryan made an appearance, as did the guilt she'd previously experienced. She realised she needed to talk it through with someone. So she turned down Jess' street and hoped she was home.

'This is a surprise,' Jess said with a smile as she opened the door. 'Or did I forget we'd organised something?'

Sophie shook her head. 'I was driving by, so I thought I'd call in.'

'I'll put the kettle on,' Jess said as she gave Sophie a hug. 'What are you doing out this way?'

As Jess made the coffees, Sophie told her about her morning with Harry.

'I'm surprised he asked you.'

'I was too.'

Then Sophie told her about the conversation with Maggie and what her thoughts had been.

Jess nodded. 'That makes sense.'

'I wasn't sure if he wanted anyone to know, so I didn't say anything beforehand. But now that we've gone, I'm sure someone saw us, so it doesn't matter if I talk about it now.'

Jess laughed. 'You said you're sure someone saw you without thinking twice. You're a local now.'

Sophie laughed as well. 'I've come to realise that everything I do will come to someone's attention at some point. And that they'll tell someone else and before I know it, I'm the topic of conversation across town, until it moves on to someone else.'

Jess smiled. 'You have been the topic of conversation lately anyway, regardless of today.'

Sophie picked up her coffee and sipped it slowly, the steam rising from the mug. 'You mean because of Ryan?'

Jess continued to smile. 'Of course because of Ryan. What else would it be? There's a lot of us who like a bit of romance.'

'I'm sure Mike can be romantic when he wants to be.'

Jess guffawed. 'I'm glad I'm sitting down. I can't remember the last time Mike did anything romantic.'

'Maybe he needs a few hints.'

'I think it will take more than a few hints. Anyway, how are things going with Ryan?'

'That's actually why I called in. I've got so many conflicting thoughts swirling around in my head that I thought talking about them might help clarify things.'

'What sort of thoughts?'

So Sophie told her how much she was enjoying being with Ryan but at the same time, she felt like she was betraying Tim, even though she knew in her heart that he'd be happy for her.

'I don't think we need to talk this through much at all.'

'What do you mean?'

'You just said the answer. You know in your heart that Tim would be happy for you. If you believe that, then you don't need to be confused.'

For the next few minutes, they sat in silence, Sophie going over what Jess had said, knowing she was right. So why couldn't she shake the feeling that she still might be doing the wrong thing. That sentiment must have been plastered across her face because Jess reached over and took hold of her hand before speaking again.

'Do you think it might be something else that's causing you to feel this way?'

Sophie looked up at Jess' face. 'Like what?'

'It's not guilt about starting over with someone else. It's guilt about having the chance to start over at all. You're still here. Tim is gone. He'll never have the chance to experience anything again. But you do.'

As soon as Jess said the words, Sophie knew she was right. It wasn't that she felt like she was being disrespectful to Tim by seeing where things might go with Ryan. It was the fact that she had her whole life in front of her, God willing, and Tim didn't. His life had been taken from him, and she was still here. She could still see the sun set of an afternoon, or watch it rise in the morning. She could still spend time with people who were important to her, could still eat delicious food, have new experiences, make plans for the future. Although, given what had happened, she was aware that her future might not be there one day, just like Tim's wasn't. But in the reverse, that future could be there. And it could take her somewhere wonderful.

Chapter Fifteen

After the visit to the cemetery, Sophie didn't see Harry for several days, which, given the size of the town was unusual. And she actually started to worry about him, something she thought she'd never do. What he needed, she'd decided, was something to occupy his mind. And so, an idea that she'd had a while ago but pushed to the back of her mind was now front and centre. All she needed to do was wait until he came back to the bookstore to mention it to him.

'Why don't you join the book club, Harry?' Sophie said to him, a few days later when he came in for a coffee.

'Isn't that just for women?'

Sophie shook her head. 'No, of course not. It's just that the women who joined were the ones who showed interest when I first brought up the idea.'

'I don't want to be the only bloke.'

'You wouldn't be. I know Jim would like to join. But he didn't want to be the only man there either. I thought maybe he'd mentioned it to you.

Harry shook his head. 'He hasn't.'

'Maybe you should start the conversation then.'

'I'll think about it.'

Sophie watched as he walked away. He'd been his usual gruff self but something in the way he said he'd think about it gave her the impression that he actually would.

And two weeks later he proved her right.

'Welcome Harry,' Catherine beamed. 'It's nice to see you here.'

Harry stood just inside the door, a copy of *The Book Thief* by Marcus Zusak in his hand. Catherine must have sold him that copy, Sophie thought. She hadn't seen Harry in the store since she'd mentioned the book club. Although, knowing him, he'd probably waited until he knew she was out, then come in to get the book, not wanting her to know until the last minute that he'd taken her advice.

Sophie beckoned to him. 'Come and grab a seat. We'll be starting as soon as everyone is here.'

Harry walked over to a chair and sat down. 'I thought I'd come and see what it's all about. If it's not too bad, I'll get Jim to come with me next time. I didn't want to bring him in case it's rubbish and he gets annoyed that I dragged him along.'

Catherine sent a stern look his way. She didn't even have to say anything. Just the look was enough.

'Sorry Sophie, shouldn't have said that,' Harry said sheepishly. 'I know you put a lot of effort into this, and from what I've heard, you all enjoy it.'

Sophie was about to respond when Bev pushed her way through the door she'd opened with her elbow and then put the food down on the table.

'Plenty to eat tonight so make sure you pile up your plates.'

Then she turned her attention to the newest book club attendee. 'Good to see you, Harry. It will be nice to hear what you thought, get a male perspective on what we've read.'

And with those words, Bev put Harry at ease. Not completely, but Sophie did notice a slight change in his demeanour. She also noticed that ever since he'd sat down, he'd been glancing at Catherine. Sophie wasn't sure if Bev had noticed but something told her that neither of them would want attention drawn to it, so she said nothing. But as she waited for the others to arrive, it occurred to her that the days Catherine hadn't come into the store recently were the same as those she hadn't seen Harry anywhere in town.

It didn't take long for the remaining members to arrive, each one taking the time to acknowledge Harry. Then Sophie explained to him how the meetings ran.

'Let's get started,' Sophie said once she'd finished. 'Who'd like to start?'

'I will,' Harry said.

Sophie turned to look at him, not expecting that he would volunteer so soon. But as she watched him, she got the feeling that he wanted to say his piece first before he lost his nerve.

'I liked it,' he pronounced. 'I liked that there were a lot of different things in the book – themes, times the story was set and types of characters.'

Catherine nodded. 'I thought the same. It made it hard to put the book down.'

As Sophie looked at Harry, waiting for him to continue, she was sure that she saw a brief smile spread across his face. Looking around the room, she didn't think anyone else had noticed.

'And I've never read a book before that was narrated by Death,' he continued.

'I haven't either,' Bev said. 'Has anyone heard of another book being narrated by Death?'

Everyone shook their heads, including Sophie. 'I know books that have been narrated by someone who has died, like

The Lovely Bones, but I haven't come across another book actually narrated by Death.'

'I found it an interesting idea,' Harry said.

'I did too,' Pam agreed. 'Although given the age of some of us in the room, there are times I wished it was narrated differently.'

Bev reached over and topped up Pam's glass. 'Have a sip of this and forget about that. We've got many years left. Strong constitutions us country women.'

Catherine smiled. 'We certainly do. Now, how about we focus on another theme from the book.'

For the rest of the meeting the discussion flowed, with everyone having plenty to say, including Harry. By the end of the night, Sophie could tell he'd had a good time. And she also noticed that on his way out, he spoke with Catherine, away from where the others could hear what they were saying.

Driving home, Sophie wondered what they'd been talking about. She knew if she asked Catherine, she wouldn't get an answer. But whatever they were talking about, Sophie couldn't help noticing that they both looked happy. And she wasn't the only one who'd noticed. Bev had also spent more than a few seconds watching them. And she'd been smiling, although she'd tried to hide it. But not before Sophie noticed.

The next day, Sophie was tired by the time she got home from the bookstore. It had been a longer day than usual with a shipment arriving early in the morning. Catherine had come in later, so Sophie unpacked the boxes and put the books on the shelf.

As well as the days she'd been away from the store, when Catherine did come in, it was long after opening time. Sophie suspected this was deliberate on Catherine's part, giving Sophie as much time alone in the store as she could, so she could see what it would be like if it was just her on her own.

And it worked, because that morning, before any customers came in, when it had been quiet, just Sophie surrounded by books, she made up her mind. This was where she was meant to be. She wasn't sure whether the bank would lend her enough money to buy the store, but she'd need to find out. Although she still had her share of the money from the sale of the house in the city, if she was going to stay, she didn't want to keep renting. She wanted a home of her own, as well as a business of her own.

'How did you go this morning?' Catherine asked as she walked in the door after lunch.

'You mean with the shipment?' Sophie said trying not to smile.

'Yes,' Catherine said slowly. 'And with anything else?'

Sophie could have made her wait but that would have been mean. So, she told Catherine her decision.

'That's wonderful,' Catherine said as she hugged her.

'Isn't that why you've been leaving me alone in the store a lot more lately? So, I could be alone and imagine what it would be like if the store was mine.'

Catherine nodded, confirming Sophie's suspicions.

'Well, it worked.'

'I hoped it would. I just had a feeling that one more day would do it. I started getting the papers ready just in case.'

Sophie looked at her, surprised. 'You were that sure I'd decide to take over the store?'

Catherine nodded. 'I've gotten to know you very well since you arrived in town. You would have tossed the idea around in your mind, unsure of which way to go, but eventually, I knew you'd come to the decision you've made.'

Sophie watched her as she said those words. Sometimes they wondered if Catherine knew her better than she knew herself.

'What's the exciting news you had to tell me in person rather than over the phone?' Jess asked as she walked into Sophie's kitchen, dropped her bag onto the bench and flopped into a chair. 'I've been curious since you texted this morning.'

Sophie paused for a moment then told her what no one else in town, apart from Catherine, knew.

'I'm buying the bookstore.'

'What!' Jess exclaimed, in a tone that almost sounded like squealing. 'I'm glad I'm sitting down.'

'Catherine told me she wanted to sell a few weeks ago and she offered it to me first.'

'I can't believe all this was going on and you never said a word.'

She paused for a moment, wondering if she'd upset Jess by not mentioning it, but the look of joy on her face told Sophie otherwise.

'I know. I thought about it a lot before deciding to do it. And it was a decision I felt I needed to come to by myself, so I hope you don't mind that I haven't said anything before this,' Sophie added, just in case she was wrong.

'Of course I don't mind,' Jess said, jumping up to give her a congratulatory hug. 'I understand that you needed to make the decision on your own.'

'It's a big commitment. And a scary one. I've never owned a business before.'

'But you've been running the store for just almost nine months now. You know what to do.'

'Yes, but what if the customers stop coming in. I'm sure some of them come in just to see Catherine.'

'And those same people will come in and see you. And buy books. And coffee and food. Just like they do now. Don't forget book club either.'

Sophie smiled, thinking about the book club. It was a highlight of her month. The members were all dear friends, even Harry, no matter how much he'd dispute that. It had brought back her love of reading as well.

'We need to celebrate,' Jess said clapping her hands together.

Sophie laughed. 'So, I guess that means the pub.'

Jess grinned. 'It's not like there's anywhere else to go. Have you told Ryan yet?'

'I was going to call him after I'd spoken to you. I know he had a busy afternoon and wouldn't be available until this evening. But if we're going to the pub, I'll see if he can join us and I'll tell him there.'

The pub was packed even though it was a Tuesday, but it was "two meals for the price of one" night.

Sophie and Jess didn't head into the bistro. Instead, Jess took Sophie to the bar and asked for two glasses of the best champagne they had. Joe the bartender laughed.

'You know we don't have any French champagne behind the bar.'

'It doesn't have to be French,' Jess said.

'Then it's sparkling wine, not champagne,' Joe replied. 'Even I know that. What do you want champagne for anyway?'

Jess looked at Sophie. 'Can I tell him?'

Sophie smiled and nodded.

'Sophie is buying the bookstore. She's staying in town.'

'That's great,' Joe said. 'And definitely worth celebrating.'

Then he turned to face the other patrons. 'Don't suppose anyone's got a bottle of fancy French fizz in their fridge?'

Surprisingly, it was Harry who answered. 'What do you want it for?'

Joe told him and Harry was silent for a moment. But then he turned towards Sophie. 'I'll go and get it.'

'What have I missed,' Ryan asked, walking up to Sophie. 'I only heard the part about fancy French fizz.'

'Sophie has some exciting news to share,' Jess burst out, before Sophie could get a word in.

Ryan turned his attention to Sophie.

'Catherine wants to retire, and she wants me to buy the bookstore. And I'm going to do it.'

Ryan didn't say anything for a moment and Sophie had the same misgivings that she'd had with Jess. Should she have mentioned to Ryan that she was thinking about it? But what she'd said to Jess was true. She had to make the decision on her own without any outside influences. So just in case, she told him the same thing she'd told Jess.

'I'm happy for you,' he said, finally. 'I guess this means you'll definitely be staying in town.'

Sophie nodded. 'Did you think I wouldn't be?'

'I wasn't sure if eventually, you'd want to go back to the city.'

Sophie shook her head. 'My home is here now. And not just because of the bookstore.'

Sophie glanced at Jess, who didn't take long to pick up on the hint. 'I'll go and grab us a table.'

It wasn't the best location, and certainly not one Sophie would have picked for this conversation, but there was nothing she could do about that now. The look of doubt on Ryan's face told her she had to say something. So she told him what she'd been feeling, and what the discussion with Jess had made clear to her. Sophie wanted to be with Ryan and to see where things could go between them.

A smile slowly spread across Ryan's face. 'That's what I want too.'

And with that, Sophie leaned over and kissed him. Behind her, she could hear cheering.

'About time Ryan shared his life with someone again,' Joe chimed in. 'And we're all happy for you too, Sophie.'

While they waited for Harry, conversation flowed around them, with everyone congratulating Sophie, saying how happy they were she was staying. As she listened to the comments and conversation, Sophie remembered her first few days in town and how she'd thought about leaving. She'd never imagined things would turn out like they had.

'About time you got back,' Joe called out when Harry walked in with the champagne.

Harry glared at him. 'I don't move as fast as I used to.'

Sophie watched as Joe opened the champagne. It had taken eight months after Tim died for her to leave her life in the city, and another nine months in Hillford, but she was finally at peace. She would never forget Tim, but she knew this was where her life was now, and also, who she wanted to share it with.

Chapter Sixteen

'I'm still not sure about this,' Jim said as he sat down, scanning the room. 'Is this really for me?'

Harry nodded. 'You're here now and I think you should stay and give it a go. You like to read, and I enjoyed the first meeting I came too. Besides, it gets us both out of our houses for a night and we've got company and people to talk to.'

Jim stared at him for a moment before responding. 'You're right. And I did make some notes about the book that I'd like to share.'

'Glad to hear it,' Sophie said as she sat down opposite them. 'And I'm glad you're both here.'

'Welcome gentlemen,' Bev declared, a few moments later as she came through the door, the last to arrive. Maggie wasn't feeling well so she'd stayed at home. 'I'm pleased you decided to join us, Jim.'

Pam, who was already seated, nodded. 'So am I.'

'Me too,' Jess chimed in, from her position next to Pam.

'Let's get started then,' Sophie said. 'What did you all think of *All The Light We Cannot See* by Anthony Doerr? Who'd like to start the discussion?

Harry turned to look at Jim. 'Why don't you go first. Get it over and done with.'

'Don't make it sound like such a chore Harry,' Bev chastised.

Harry scowled. 'I didn't mean it that way. I just meant it's the first book club he's been to so he's a bit nervous.'

'I think everyone can tell I'm a bit nervous Harry,' Jim said to his friend. 'But I'd rather someone else go first, just so I get the idea. I might have written notes about the wrong things.'

Sophie smiled. 'There is no such thing Jim. What we talk about is based on our own thoughts, our own opinions of the book. There is no right or wrong.'

Jim nodded. 'That's good to know. But I'd still like someone else to go first.'

'I will,' Bev said, surprising no one in the room.

So the meeting began, and continued for longer than usual, mostly because Jim and Harry wouldn't stop talking.

Jim hadn't been joking when he said he'd written some notes. He had several pages of the notebook he'd brought with him filled with his observations about the characters, the themes, even the locations. And with everything he said, Harry had something to add. If Sophie hadn't jumped in every now and then to ask someone else a direct question, the others wouldn't have had a chance to get a word in.

But Sophie could tell that no one minded. That all the other book club members would have been happy to just sit and listen. Jim was more animated than Sophie had ever seen him, and she'd never heard him talk so much. The more he talked, the more the others could see that he was enjoying himself. They could tell that Harry was enjoying himself too, so, no one wanted to stop either of them. And it was also clear how much of an effort they'd both put in.

Watching them as they spoke had put a smile on Sophie's face. On Catherine's as well, particularly when it was Harry who had he floor.

'So, what did you think?' Sophie asked Jim as everyone was packing up.

'I liked it, more than I thought I would.'

'Does that mean you'll be back next month?'

Jim nodded. 'I'll be here.'

As he walked out the door, Sophie was glad that she'd suggested he come along. It had been good for him. Good for Harry too. As with the last book club, Harry and Catherine had another conversation away from the others. This time, it wasn't just herself and Bev who noticed. The others did too. They also noticed Catherine reach out and touch Harry's hand before he turned to say goodnight to those still there.

'So, today is the day,' Ryan said as they sat on Sophie's front verandah eating breakfast, Molly running around in the yard in front of them. After realising that she wouldn't be getting any of their food that is.

When Ryan wasn't around, Sophie sometimes gave Molly treats from her plate. It wasn't something he would do, as he thought it encouraged bad habits. There had already been several conversations on how he believed dogs were working animals and should stay outside.

But it was Sophie's house and Molly spent as much time inside as she did outside, although, given the size Molly was getting, that might not be practical for much longer. The thought of leaving her outside all the time wasn't something Sophie was comfortable with, so she'd have to figure out a way to still let Molly in without her destroying the house through her exuberance.

'Yes, I've got an appointment with the solicitor at 9 am.'

'It's a big step.'

Sophie nodded. 'It is, but I'm ready. To own the store and this house, as well as build a life here with you.'

They sat in comfortable silence while they finished eating, then after breakfast, Ryan dropped Sophie into town. He'd already organised a celebration for later that day. He wouldn't tell her what it was. He wanted it to be a surprise. But he said he would drive her home afterwards so there was no need for her to bring her car into town.

By 9.30 am, all the papers were signed and Sophie walked slowly back to the bookstore, taking the time to let it sink in that it was officially hers. She was the proprietor of The Book Haven, as well as the owner of a farmhouse. She'd briefly toyed with the idea of changing the name of the store but decided against it. Everyone knew it by that name, and she wanted to keep the connection with all that Catherine had created and built up over the years. And besides, she couldn't think of a more fitting name. A haven was what it had been for her, almost since the first day she'd arrived.

For the rest of the day, Sophie was run off her feet. So many people came in to say congratulations and to buy coffees, food and lots of books. The support was amazing, and she was so grateful that she had so many caring people around her, people who were thrilled she was now a permanent part of this town.

Bev and Jess had prepared extra food, knowing the townspeople would turn up. They'd both agreed to continue supplying the store with food, which Sophie was pleased about as the three of them worked well together in keeping the customers well fed. It was one of the many things at the store that she didn't want to change.

There were only a couple of things she did want to change. One of them was update some of the systems Catherine had been using. They'd worked well, but technology had moved on. Catherine had never shown any interest; she was happy using what she had been for past several years. But Sophie wanted a more modern system to manage orders and deliveries, and she'd already done some research on what she wanted to implement. Now that the store was hers, it was on the top of her list.

She also wanted to get some new furniture. What was there was serviceable, but not always comfortable, especially if you were sitting for a long time. Something the book club members had mentioned once or twice. Besides, more comfortable chairs would encourage people to stay longer and maybe spend some more money, something she had to think about now that she had a loan to pay back.

By closing time, Sophie was tired and all she wanted to do was sit down. Then she remembered that Ryan had something planned so she started to pack up the few items that were still in the food cabinet to put them in the fridge.

'I'd leave those there if I were you. You'll need them soon.'

Sophie turned around to see Ryan grinning, standing in the doorway.

'What will I need these for? If they don't go in the fridge overnight, I'll have to throw them out and I don't want to waste them.'

'They won't go to waste,' Bev said as she came in for the second time that day with her arms full.

Behind her was Jess, also carrying food for the second time that day, followed by Maggie, Pam, Jim and Harry. Catherine was the last to come in. For a moment, Sophie was worried she might be sad that the store was no longer hers. But a smile and a long hug from Catherine put that thought out of her mind.

'What are you all doing here?' Sophie asked, surprised to see them.

From behind his back, Ryan produced two bottles of champagne. 'They're here for your first day as the owner. It only seemed fitting that you celebrate with the book club members.'

Sophie was chuffed. She had no idea this is what Ryan had been planning but it was perfect.

'Where did you find those? After the night at the pub, I thought Harry was the only person in town who had a bottle of fancy French fizz as Joe calls it.'

Ryan laughed too. 'He might call it that, but he knew where to order them from. Is it too early for a toast?'

Sophie shook her head. 'Not for an occasion like this. I don't have any champagne glasses here though.'

Ryan smiled. 'Good thing I brought those with me too.'

Ryan opened the bottles and poured everyone a glass. He then raised his glass. 'To Sophie.'

'To Sophie,' the others echoed.

As the food was passed around, and glasses topped up again from the extra bottles that Maggie and Pam had brought, Sophie took the time to talk to everyone and thank them for the support they'd given her, not only when she was the new person in town, but by agreeing to become part of the book club, the thing that had first made her feel like she belonged. The last person she spoke to was Harry.

'I know you and I didn't get off to a good start.'

Sophie was about to say something when he continued.

'I know that was my fault. But I'm glad we've moved on from that, and I'm glad you're here and you're staying.'

Ryan smiled. 'I'm glad she's staying too.'

Sophie smiled back at him, and at Harry. 'So am I.'

Chapter Seventeen

As Sophie jumped out of bed, she was excited that show day was finally here. Ryan was already up and about; he was a much earlier riser than she was. Even after all the time she'd spent in Hillford, that was one thing that was not going to change.

'Morning,' he said, as she walked into the kitchen. 'I've made breakfast.'

Ryan had gotten over his initial hesitation at cooking for Sophie. He'd been worried that what he prepared would not be as good as what she'd cooked for him. But Sophie had assured him it was. Or it would be once she gave him a few more pointers. Not that she told him that. One step at a time.

As Sophie looked out the window, she was happy to see a bright, sunny day with no hint of rain clouds. A perfect summer day.

'We'll have to leave in about forty-five minutes to get to the showgrounds on time for the pre-show briefing,' Ryan said, dishing up the omelette he'd made.

'I'll be ready,' Sophie said. 'I'll eat this then shower and get dressed. We'll grab Molly on the way out.'

Arriving at the showground, Sophie could see people already milling around, setting up the display spaces and food outlets. Molly jumped out as soon as Sophie opened the car door and ran towards Jess who was waving.

'Morning,' Jess said as she hugged Sophie, something that made Molly jump up and down as if to tell them she was missing out.

So Jess reached down and gave Molly another pat. 'I think she's as excited as we are.'

Sophie laughed. 'Yes, she is. Look at all these people she can get pats from.'

Jess laughed too. 'Wait until some of the animals get here. Molly won't know what to do with herself.'

As Sophie walked around the site, saying hello to everyone she came across, she was thrilled that her idea had come to life. Everyone she saw was smiling and doing all they could to get everything ready in time for the gates to open.

'Hello Sophie,' Jim said, walking towards her with a clipboard in his hand.

'Morning Jim. How's everything going?'

'Coming together nicely. Everyone on the committee has completed all the tasks they were set. And not just completed, everyone went above and beyond.'

Sophie smiled. 'I'm glad to hear it. Now, I better go and get the food stalls ready.'

Jim nodded. 'Thanks again for taking charge of that. Now, where did Ryan go? I've got a few things to go over with him.'

Sophie pointed to her left to where Ryan was standing and Jim headed towards him, a resolve in his step.

As Sophie turned back, she could see Bev heading towards her. And behind her, rides were being erected, ready to delight the children, as well as the young at heart later in the day.

'I can't believe how many rides you've organised, Bev. Where did they all come from?'

'One of my cousins used to work on the show circuit many years ago. He still has contacts, so he put me on to the right people.'

'That's fantastic.'

Bev nodded. 'Yes, but what's also fantastic was how enthusiastic the ride operators were to be involved once I explained why we were holding the show.'

Sophie laughed. 'I'm sure there was some persuasion on your part as well.'

Bev smiled. 'Maybe a little bit. Right, I can't stand here talking all day. I want to make sure everything is ready for opening time.'

Sophie watched as Bev walked off, although it wasn't so much walking as striding with purpose.

Behind her, Ryan came up and put his arm around her shoulder.

'Did Jim let you know what he wanted you to do?'

Ryan nodded. 'I'm on my way to do that now. I just wanted to let you know that I've organised some of the volunteers to bring the food from the ute to the stalls.'

Not only had Ryan helped her prepare and pack the food, but he'd also scrounged several transportable refrigerated units that he'd loaded on to the back of his ute. Between what they'd prepared and what the other women of the CWA cooking committee had prepared, no one would be going hungry.

'Morning Sophie, morning Ryan,' Catherine's voice called out.

They turned to see where she was and were surprised to see Harry carrying a pile of quilts so high, they almost couldn't see his face.

'Take them over to the shed on the left Harry,' Catherine instructed. 'That's the last of the quilts that have been entered into the competition. The others are already displayed, ready for the judging.'

'How many entries did you get?' Sophie asked, watching as Harry struggled to walk and not drop anything.

Ryan watched him too, then hurried after Harry and grabbed some of the quilts to carry, before continuing on to do what Jim had asked of him.

'Forty entries.'

'Really?' Sophie said, surprised. 'I didn't realise that many people in town quilted.'

Catherine shook her head. 'They don't. We've had entries from all over the district, even some from towns one hundred kilometres away.'

'That's amazing.'

Catherine nodded. 'And that's not all. We've had a similar number of cakes entered and they came from far and wide as well.'

'With that kind of interest, maybe we should have organised a few more competitions.'

Catherine smiled. 'I did. I discussed it with Jim and then added a home-grown vegetable competition, a jams and marmalade competition and a plant competition.'

As she listened to Catherine, Sophie realised she should have known that's what would happen. Catherine loved this town and the more she could get people involved, the more she would make it happen.

'Have you seen Maggie?' Sophie asked, looking around her.

Catherine pointed to her right. 'She's over there talking to the fireworks operators.'

'I didn't know we were having fireworks.'

Catherine nodded. 'Maggie offered to help with that as well as the other things she put her name down for. She's organised all sorts of entertainment, both for daytime and night-time. I can't remember the last time I saw fireworks.'

Sophie could. It had been with Tim. But this time, the memory didn't cause her pain. Instead, she smiled. She was lucky to have experienced what she had with Tim. Not everyone got to have a relationship like they'd had. And now there was the possibility that she'd have not one, but two relationships like that. She was very lucky indeed.

From the minute the gates opened to the last of the fireworks exploding in the night sky, the show was a success. The crowds kept coming all day, and laughter and screams of delight filled the air. Sophie couldn't have imagined a better day. Jess won the cake competition, which surprised no one. And Pam came first in the quilting competition. Jim had entered his home-grown vegetables and won a prize. Even Harry had a ribbon to take home, for his homemade rosella jam, which was a surprise to Sophie. She had no idea he could make jam.

'There's a lot you, and others, don't know about him,' Catherine said when Sophie mentioned it to her.

'What else can you share that I don't know?' Sophie asked, hoping Catherine would reveal what Sophie had been wondering about.

But Catherine remained quiet, so Sophie was still left speculating about what exactly was going on between the two of them.

By mid-afternoon, almost everyone in town had been through the gates. And some from out of town, including Pam's daughter Cara and her family.

'Nice to meet you,' Sophie said, taking note of how much she looked like her mum. 'Pam has told me so much about you.'

'Nice to meet you too. Mum has told me a lot about you as well.'

Sophie was surprised and wondered why she'd come up in conversation between the two of them.

'There you are,' Pam said, walking up to them. 'I've been looking for you.'

'I was interested to meet the person you keep talking about,' Cara said, putting her arm around her mum's shoulders.

Pam laughed. 'I talk about her because we're all glad she came to our little town and decided to stay. And that she started the book club that I enjoy so much.'

Sophie was touched. Even though she now felt like Hillford was where she belonged, it was nice to still hear from others that she was considered part of the town.

'I'm glad you got to meet Sophie, but I'm going to have to drag you away. Your children want you to go on a ride with them and I said I'd find you.'

Cara turned to look at her mum. 'What sort of ride?'

Pam laughed again. 'Nothing scary. Just the dodgem cars.'

Cara then turned to look at Sophie. 'Even that's scary at my age.'

Sophie laughed. 'If I went on those, I'd probably have to see a physiotherapist afterwards.'

'Let's hope I don't! It was great talking with you, Sophie, even though it was only briefly.'

'Hopefully I'll get to see you before you head home.'

Cara nodded. 'I'd like that.'

As she walked away, arm in arm with Pam, Sophie was pleased to see how happy they both looked.

When the last of the fireworks faded into the night, Sophie took a moment to take everything in, all the components of the day. And all the joy she'd seen on people's faces. She'd come a long way, but she was home. There was only one more thing she needed to do to make her life in Hillford complete. Return to the city one last time, then come back, leaving the past behind.

Chapter Eighteen

As Sophie walked around the house she now owned, she couldn't imagine living anywhere else. Walking from room to room, she took in every aspect of the changes she'd made and wherever she walked, Molly followed. It was her home too.

The last room she came to was the dining room, and as she contemplated what was in front of her, she realised something wasn't quite right and it took her a moment to figure out what it was. The walls were bare. And Sophie knew just what to hang. She went to the box she'd put in the cupboard in the spare room on the first day she'd arrived and pulled out the painting Tim had done of her. After she'd hung it, she stood back and stared at it. It was her but it wasn't. So many things had changed since it had been painted. She wasn't that person anymore. But that was ok. She was happy with who she was now.

Sophie headed into the kitchen and pulled a recipe book off the shelf. Which recipe would she choose? She had many favourites in this particular book, as had Tim. Back and forth, she went, turning the pages, until she decided. With the warmer weather, she picked creamy Tuscan garlic prawns, with a crispy mushroom parmigiana salad. For dessert, she would follow up with passionfruit sorbet. She made a list of ingredients and headed into town, hoping Maggie would have everything she needed in stock.

'Morning,' Sophie said as she walked in. 'I better do a good job of this dinner.'

Maggie gave her hand a squeeze, knowing how important tonight was. 'It will be the best meal you've ever cooked. I'm so glad things are working out.'

Sophie smiled. 'So am I.'

Fifteen minutes later, Sophie had everything she needed. Except the passionfruit.

'Lucky I've got some at home,' Maggie said. 'Call in on the way back to your place and grab some off our vine.'

With the ingredients gathered and now spread across the kitchen bench, Sophie began to work. An hour passed and she didn't even notice. Chopping, mixing, marinating, it was very soothing, and she lost herself in the preparation. It wasn't until Ryan arrived that she realised she better get a move on and get ready herself.

'Welcome,' Sophie said as Catherine and Harry walked in her front door. 'Glad you could come.'

Catherine smiled. 'Neither of us would pass up an opportunity to eat anything you cooked.'

Sophie smiled too. 'That's lovely of you to say. Ryan is opening a wine. We can either stay inside or sit on the verandah. What would you prefer?'

'The verandah would be nice,' Catherine said. 'We can watch the sunset. What do you think, Harry?'

'Good idea,' he said as he turned around and headed back towards the door. But not before he reached out and took Catherine's hand.

It had taken some persuading, but Catherine had finally come clean. It wasn't a grand romance or anything like that, she stressed. But they enjoyed each other's company, and at this point in their lives, they both liked the idea of caring about someone else. They had a gentle affection for each other was how Catherine described it. And Sophie was thrilled for both of them.

Over dinner, Sophie couldn't believe the change she saw in Harry. He looked truly happy, something Sophie hadn't seen before. But she knew as well as anyone that if someone could make an impact on a life, it was Catherine.

As the sun began to rise the following morning, Sophie hopped out of bed, leaving Ryan to sleep. It was the only time since they'd been together that she'd woken before he did. She got dressed quietly, jumped in her car and headed down the driveway. She'd told Ryan her plans earlier in the week and reminded him again the previous evening after Catherine and Harry left. He thought what she was doing would be good for her. Even if he hadn't, she would have gone through with her plans anyway, but it was nice that he supported her. He planned to use the time to finish the last minor repair at the house. And, Sophie suspected, play with Molly. The more time he'd spent at her house, the less he mentioned that dogs belonged outside.

She hadn't told anyone from her previous life that she was coming. It wasn't that she didn't want to see anyone, but for this first visit back, she needed to see things by herself. It felt like she was saying goodbye to Tim. He would always be part of her life, always in her heart, but if she was going to move on, she needed to do something to signify the change. Something tangible. So here she was, on her way.

The drive was uneventful, and she enjoyed the time alone in the car. She thought back to her drive out to Hillford, how she'd felt, the grief, the uncertainty. She'd come a long way, emotionally as well as in distance.

As she got to the outskirts of the city and the traffic became heavier, she realised she didn't miss this part at all. She was used to Hillford with its quiet roads, without a traffic light in sight.

Her first stop was the beach. That was something she did miss. When she'd lived here, she'd swum in the ocean all throughout summer. It was summer now and while she enjoyed swimming in the dam in Hillford, it wasn't quite the same as having the waves wash over her. She changed into her togs and slowly walked down to the water, feeling the soft, warm sand beneath her toes. She paused for a moment, digging her feet in until they were covered and watched the waves, one by one, rolling towards the shore in perfect lines.

From the moment she ducked under the first wave, she felt the disquiet that had been drifting through her mind since she decided to come back wash away in the cool salt water. She stayed longer than she intended to, diving under or jumping over the waves, her energy levels rising with each minute. By the time she walked from the ocean, she felt different. And ready to drive down her old street.

The house looked exactly the same. As Sophie stood across the road, she wondered whether that was because the new owners liked what she and Tim had done or whether they just hadn't got around to changing anything yet. Whatever the reason, she was glad it still looked the same. She wasn't sure how she would have felt if it looked different and there was no tangible reminder of what she and Tim had done together.

Luckily, it was the middle of the day and no one was home. She wasn't ready to see who was living in the house and she wasn't ready to talk to any of the neighbours. They'd got on well while she'd been here, but they knew what had happened and they'd ask questions, which she didn't want to answer. She didn't want to bring her new life into her old one.

Sophie didn't stay long. It was too sad. But also clarifying. This was no longer her home. She had a new home.

Before she left the city, there was one last thing Sophie needed to do.

She parked her car and headed down the path. She was alone, which surprised her. Previous times when she'd been here, other mourners had been present, at other gravesites. People she'd glanced at, just for a few seconds. Long enough to notice they had the same look on their faces that she did. A look that she couldn't conceal. Make-up didn't hide grief.

But today there was no one. She continued walking until she reached her destination. She could see that Tim's mother had been there recently because there were fresh flowers. His mum was the one person she'd contacted to say she was coming. They had always gotten on well and it would have been nice to see her. However, his mum had already organised a trip to visit Tim's sister, and she'd left the previous day.

It doesn't say much about a life, Sophie thought to herself as she looked at the headstone. 'Beloved son and fiancé'. Sophie wished it said more, but at the time, neither she nor his mother could find any words. Tim couldn't be shrunk to only a few words. They would need pages to capture everything. Maybe now that she was in a better place, she'd reach out to Tim's mum again and between them they could get the wording changed.

Sophie stayed for a few more minutes before heading back to her car. It was time to go.

As Sophie drove back into town, she felt a sense of calm come over her. A town like Hillford was not somewhere she ever expected to live. But now it was home. On the outskirts of town, she pulled over. In front of her stood the Welcome to Hillford sign, which now read, *Population 1564.*

Shelley Banks is a passionate writer who enjoys creating a story that will entertain readers. She is the author of three full-length novels - *One Weekend, The Diary and the Green Dress, The Long Way Around* and *Finding Home.* She is also the author of five fiction and non-fiction short reads, perfect for when you're short on time - *Short, Sweet and September – volumes 1,2,3,4,5.*

She is also the author of September Sprouts (septembersprouts.wordpress.com), a fiction and non-fiction blog that aims to encourage people to read.

Shelley lives in Gordon Park, Queensland, Australia.

facebook.com/writershellb/
instagram.com/writershellb/